MW01134707

WHEN BOYS
BECOME MEN

WHEN BOYS BECOME MEN

Santiago Dizon

Library of Congress Control Number:		2020916193
ISBN:	Hardcover	978-1-6641-2705-0
	Softcover	978-1-6641-2704-3
	eBook	978-1-6641-2703-6

Print information available on the last page.

Rev. date: 10/29/2020

To order additional copies of this book, contact:
Xlibris
844-714-8691
www.Xlibris.com
Orders@Xlibris.com
817516

Praise for *When Boys Become Men* by Santiago Dizon

"Gotta read it one of these days."
Sister

"At least this project kept him out of the bars for a while."
Gary Schwab

"I remember when Santiago got in a fight with Dick Christianson right in the middle of the crosswalk at Hoover High School. Dick said there was no Santa Claus and Santiago slugged 'em. Sorry, what was the question again?"
Principal Mr. McMasters

"Nice little book to take along when camping.
Don't forget the matches."
Johnny Lopez

"I knew he deserved that 'C' grade I gave him in English."
Mrs. Judy Davis

"Santiago was so proud to have graduated in the top eighty-fifth of his class. *When Men Become Boys* proves he deserved his ranking."
Classmate

History is not there for you to like or dislike. It is there to learn from. And if it offends you, even the better because then you are less likely to repeat it. It's not yours to erase. It belongs to all of us!

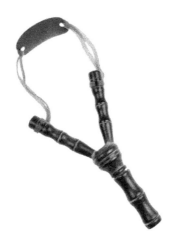

FOR

Sweet Shirley Mae
&
Nate the Great
&
Doug Munro Anderson

PREFACE

Joanne Keliher, the girl next door, muchas gracias for your help. Thank you, George Keliher for keeping this machine alive over and over again. And Richard Reinbolt, the most inspirational guy I know, thanks for your encouragement through the years.

California, here I come
Right back where I started from
Where bowers are flowers bloom in the spring
Each morning at dawning
Birdies sing and everything
A sun kissed miss said, "Don't be late!"
That's why I can hardly wait
Open up that Golden Gate!
California, here I come!
California, here I come, yeah!

Earthquakes and droughts are part of the scene
And the sun will do damage without sunscreen,
Yosemite, Sequoia, redwood and surf
Where on this earth has a grander turf?

WHO IS REAL?

Meriwether Lewis, explorer
William Clark, explorer
Gabriel Moraga, explorer
Sacagawea, guide
John Colter, mountain man
John Potts, mountain man
Jedediah Smith, mountain man
Thomas Fitzpatrick, mountain man
Hugh Glass, mountain man
Kit Carson, mountain man
Jim Bridger, mountain man
Jim Beckwourth, mountain man
Kintpuash, Modoc
Scarface Charley, Modoc
Shaknasty Jim, Modoc
Donners', immigrants
Frederick Douglass, statesman
John Muir, naturalist
Jessie Benton Freemont, naturalist
Josiah Whitney, geologist
Juan Jose Dominguez, explorer
Joseph Walker, explorer
Juan Rodriguez, explorer
Richard Owens, guide
Buffalo Hump, Comanche chief
Tecumseh, Shawnee Chief
The Prophet, Shawnee shaman
Junipero Serra, missionary
Marcus Whitman, missionary
Pio Pico, governor
Peter Burnett, governor
John Augustus Sutter, colonizer

John C. Freemont, army officer
James W. Marshall, carpenter
Samuel Brannan, 49er
Anton Roman, 49er
Ah Toy, soiled dove
Joaquin Murrieta, rebel
Juan Flores, rebel
Salomon Pico, rebel
Snowshoe Thompson, mailman
Brigham Young, Mormon prophet
Leland Stanford, businessman
Collis Huntington, businessman
Mark Hopkins, businessman
Charles Crocker, businessman
Henry Harrison, 9th president
James Polk, 11th president
Abraham Lincoln, 13th president
James Garfield, 20th president
William McKinley, 25th president
Theodore Roosevelt, 26th president
Wm. Bryan, presidential candidate
E. Debs, presidential candidate
Santa Anna, Mexican president
Juan Cabrillo, sea captain
John Phillips, sea captain
Juan Jose Dominguez, land baron
Manuel Rodriguez, mayor
Fred Eaton, mayor
Phinneas Banning, investor
John Downey, investor
Griffith J. Griffith, philanthropist
Harrison Otis, publisher

Harry Chandler, publisher
Theodore Judah, engineer
William Mulholland, engineer
J.B. Lippencott, engineer
William Wolfskill, agriculturist
S.W. Griffith, film director
Fielding Yost, football coach
Ralph Fischer, football player
Samuel Clemons, author
Richard Henry Dana Jr., author
Las Sergas de Esplandian, author
Xianfeng, emperor

BOOK ONE

WHEN BOYS BECOME MEN

CHAPTER ONE

Amerca had itchy feet in the 1840's, Oregon and California were yawning. Mountain Men, who were searching for beaver, prompted the way. However, the fur trade was waning, that rodent mostly harvested and fashion in Europe now favored silk hats. For more than two decades, characters like Jedediah Smith, Jim Bridges, "Broken Hand" Fitzpatrick and Kit Carson explored, trapped and later guided folks through the Rockies, folks keen for a place of their own.

From sea to shining sea, Manifest Destiny was on a roll!

The problem was the collision. Lakota, Shoshone, Comanche, Nez Perce, Ute, Arapaho, Paiute, Bannock, Crow and Gross Ventre were only a handful of nations displaced, the Native American soon to be history. The People, sovereign in their nature, were not exactly Rousseau's 'Noble Savage'. Indians were warriors, who stole their neighbor's horses and captured slaves. But it was *their* way of life.

The old soldier, soaking in the cool winter's sun, dozed outside Mr. Darling's sundry store with his hat shading his face.

Walking by the store, Jarrett spied his friend, "Hey Sergeant, got time? How 'bout a story for me?"

Amos Crabtree, retired U.S. Army sergeant was rich with anecdotes and more than willing and anxious to share his treasures. "Didn't mean to wake you Sarge but golly it's good to see you."

"That's okay, Jarrett, sit yourself down on the bench here. Thought you might be over at the corral or blacksmithing. You seem to grow a couple inches every time we howdy. Ever tell you 'bout the time ol' 'Broken Hand' was running from them Ventres in South Pass? Or maybe how Tom's hair turned at only thirty years, we're talkin' pure white!" Without waiting for the answer, Amos continued. Jarrett knew the yarns, exciting his imagination.

"Let's see, yup, been nearly fifteen years now, or fourteen, don't matter much, it's a way back anyway."

The sergeant's tales about California with Jedediah Smith and Tom "Broken Hand" Fitzpatrick stirred Jarrett's juices.

Stories were exciting, but Jarrett yearned for his own. Orphaned at twelve, he slept on his pallet above Munro Arnold's blacksmith rafters with all that sweet-smelling hay. The sergeant's Mountain Men, heroes in Jarrett's dreams.

Meals, taken with the smith and his wife Lenni Mae, were traded for chores and Jarrett was learning the trade as well. Mrs. Arnold taught him letters and how to figure numbers.

Sharing his plans with the old soldier, Jarrett was ready to challenge his fancies with action.

"What should I take with me, Sergeant? Don't have much. Pa left me an ol' haversack, my moccasins are good and even have an extra pair. Got my slingshot too, so I can knock down a bird or a rabbit."

"Goin' alone, Jarrett?"

"That kid Noah, he might want to come along. Got no folks. Does odd jobs all over town, nothing steady. Seems real smart, always reading something or other. I'm seventeen now and it's my time to, what do ya call it, Sarge?"

"See the elephant."

"That's it, gotta go see the elephant."

"Slow down boy, thought 'bout where you wanna go?"

"Sure have, I wan…..no, I need to go where you went with Mr. Smith and Mr. Fitzgerald. California!"

"Fitzpatrick, son, not Fitzgerald."

"You opened the door for me Sarge, have to see for myself."

Later in the day, after finishing up around the stables, Jarrett wandered down Main, San Luis' only street. At the bottom by the stream, he found Noah.

"Watcha doing, Noah?"

"Sitting here thinking 'bout things and whittling this ol' branch. Was busy earlier though, skipping some rocks in the stream."

"Wadaya been thinking?"

"Taking my leave soon, don't know where to. Gotta' do more than work odd jobs, skip rocks and whittle branches."

"Want to go see the elephant?"

"Sure, where and when?"

"California! Reckon we could start in a month. The snow will be mostly melted and that'll gives us some time to collect our possibles. It's a far piece. Been talking with ol' Sarge."

"Now that's a fine notion, Jarrett. Should have most of these branches trimmed away by then."

Jarrett, just for fun, skipped a rock of his own and headed home. "Mrs. Arnold, I got something to tell ya."

"Why you haven't called me Mrs. Arnold for three years, did you break something?"

"Nah, just a little nervous."

"Why, are you courting that pretty little Maryalice?"

"This is more important than girls, Lenni Mae."

"Well then, come in and sit yourself in the parlor and I'll bring some cookies, be just a minute."

"These are your favorites, molasses and walnuts. Okay my boy, what's the big secret?"

"I'm going to California, me and Noah."

"Goodness Jarrett, what do you know 'bout the road? Do you know the way? How will you get there? What ever will you take with you? Why don't you just stay here with Munro and me?"

"You've made me feel at home here Lenni Mae, but it's just something I gotta' do. Maybe I'm a gypsy or something."

"Here comes the man of the house now, must be time for supper. Has Jarrett told you about his plans?"

"No, what are you thinking son?"

"Heading to California in three weeks and I want to thank you and Lenni Mae. You saved me. If you hadn't taken me in, I'd be sleeping in the streets. Just something I gotta do. If I don't go, I'll always wonder, always, just gotta go. Been talking with Sergeant Crabtree all 'bout it."

"Did the sarge tell you how the Spaniards arrested him, the whole shebang of them."

"He did Munro, they let them go after some talking."

"What's your first move, Jarrett?"

"Noah and I are going together, seems a real capable guy. Sergeant Crabtree thinks we could hike about two hundred miles north on that trail to Denver and work for some time, make some money to buy our goods. Then join one of those wagon trains that are going west."

"Munro tell him he's welcome to stay with us. We want him to stay here."

"You're always welcome, Jarrett. We both knew your ma and pa and they'd sure be proud of you."

"Munro and I are partial to you Jarrett, you've become part of our family."

"See your serious about this. Tell you what; tomorrow morning, go over to Mr. Darling's and buy some round shot for a Hawken's fifty-four caliber and get two boxes with powder. See that muzzle-loader and powder horn hanging above the door. Tell Mr. Darling to put it on my bill. You and I are goin' out the back a ways and practice tomorrow."

Jarrett was there before Mr. Darling opened his door. An hour later, they placed a dozen old bottles on stumps and fallen trees fifty yards away.

"Okay Jarrett, this piece weighs fifteen pounds, a bit clumsy, but you seem to be comfortable handling it. Got your hands on it good and seems snug in your shoulder, not too tight, comfortable. Aim at one of the targets, that's it. How does it feel, maybe your off hand out a little more, there that looks 'bout right. You're the one's gotta shoot. You know how to adjust the sight?"

"Dang, Munro, got some kick to it. Might've held it a mite too loose." Twelve bottles still standing proud.

"You almost winged that crow flying over. This time space your feet a little more apart, remember your breathing. Breath in, hold it, half out, hold and squeeze the trigger slowly. Get comfortable with it. Pretend you're handling a woman, firm but gentle."

Before noon, all the bottles were shattered and replaced with pinecones. Jarrett had the basics, finishing the second box of shot from a hundred yards.

"These Hawkins supposed to hit their targets from almost a quarter mile, that's what those ol' timers say."

"This one's yours now Jarrett. Always keep it clean and hope you never have to use it for anything but meat."

CHAPTER TWO

January 1847

The sky was just fixing itself, like it usually does. This morning mostly gray with rumors of pink, quickly turning red. Following the wagon road down the hill from San Luis at 7,500 feet, their first challenge was to meet the trail to Denver, then hike straight north. They both knew they had a long way to go, but California was a strong magnet. A great adventure for the boys, soon to become men. It was late March.

True to form, Jarrett brought down rabbits and squirrels; Noah had cooking fires ready.

Emptying their packs, they again inventoried their necessaries: each had a knife and whetstone, one slingshot between them, a few feet of rope, flint and a bit of steel for fire making, the Hawkins, three boxes of shot and powder, cleaning oil and rags, a cooking pot, a grill, a sack of salt and their personals. They cleaned their teeth with twigs, with a bit of salt and charcoal from their fires.

"One good thing Jarrett, our pack's not too heavy. Think we're going to make it. Nice of the sergeant to gift us these knives, must have used them in his army days."

"The Arnolds' gave us two weeks of staples to start us out. Got the Hawkins, too. Gotta admit they're not easy to handle and wouldn't have enough time to load and prime if a big ol' griz said hello."

"Did Sarge ever tell you 'bout that big brown that almost ate Jed Smith? Can you imagine going around with all those scars and an ear hanging loose?"

"Reckon I'd grow my hair long."

On their third night out after they were under their blankets,

Jarrett asked, "You ever wonder 'bout those stars? Look far away, further than California even."

"A bit, yeah. I dunno, like to think that maybe they're campfires of folks who have died." Noah sat up and continued, "See that bright star up there, kinda by itself? To your left side a little more."

"Yup. What's special 'bout that one?"

"Maybe that one's the campfire of my folks, looking down at me at night, kinda saying howdy."

"That's real nice, Noah. I'm going to look for my folks. Your star is the one Sarge told us to look for to know which way we're going. Sarge said that's always north."

"Well, that makes it really easy to find California, Jarrett."

"G'night. We got another big day tomorrow."

The third night on the trail, Jarrett asked, "Noah, what's your last name, never knew."

"Me neither, not really Jarrett. I was little when Mr. and Mrs. Pawley took me in. Told me my folks got killed in a fire. Said I could use their name, Pawley, so that's it I reckon. But, not really my name."

After some time, Jarrett said, "Want to use my name, Andersen? Be like having a brother. Supposed to come from Norway, that's over there in Europe."

"That's good of you Jarrett. Noah Andersen, sound's real good. Noah Andersen, yeah, real nice. Thanks."

After three weeks and two hundred twenty-six miles on the trail, they approached the outskirts of Denver where they found jobs at Whalen's Stables, mucking, feeding, watering and grooming the horses. Whalen's specialized in breaking and training horses for the small holdings outside of town. The boss, Chris Whalen, was craggy-faced, tall and bowlegged, an easy goin' kind of guy.

Two weeks of regular routine was broken one morning when one of the cowboys, too drunk to work, stayed abed in the bunkhouse. Noah, the slightly taller of the two, was offered the task of breaking his first horse, a skinny brown and white pinto filly about a year old. She looked tired and was saddled and ready to go. Tossed three times, Noah climbed back on each time, impressing Chris with his sand. The boss figured right; the boy was raw but he himself had started the same way. Hell, all the cowboys had started pretty much the same.

"Good job Noah, think you'll make a cowboy. How 'bout you Jarrett, wanna go?"

What else could he say? "Yessir Mr. Whalen, I'll try", bluffing himself as well. Jarrett had studied the real cowboys at work, who now gathered around to watch, knowing he was green. A cowboy brought out another filly, this one without saddle.

He gentled the strawberry roan pony, first showing her, then touching her with blanket and rope. After some time, he haltered her and led her around. Slowly, he introduced her to the bridle and bit, more leading, more touching and complements the whole time.

"That's a good girl, yes my beauty!" Next, speaking softly, always touching and after some time put on the blanket, then the saddle and stirrups and cinched it up.

Jarrett thought that was the way he remembered the cowboys doing it. Reflecting a moment, he put his foot in the stirrup and seated himself. The horse was calm, a natural to the saddle. Relieved, the new cowboy relaxed. Then, that sweet little mare exploded, throwing Jarrett and trotting away, showing off to the giggling cowboys. Embarrassed and a little mad, Jarrett climbed aboard once more. Another ejection and then another. Finally, a partnership between the two, horse and cowboy.

On their time off, the two pals explored fast-growing Denver, partial to the Mexican enclave. For one thing, it was cheap. They tried their first cerveza and the señoritas darn pretty as well. Sitting outside El Tepeyac, they again talked about California.

"Took us three weeks to get to Denver and California's a lot further. Just wondering how much longer we oughta work here? How much more we need to save?"

"You know Noah, in a couple weeks we might've enough to buy a couple good horses and tack as well. And a rifle for you? I was looking in some stores last week. Maybe we could buy a used Henry, be good to have one of those new repeaters. I didn't tell ya' that Munro gave me a twenty-dollar gold coin as well as the Hawken. I'll throw that in. Denver has treated us really good. Glad you're still thinking California though."

"Must be June next week. If we're goin', we better git." Pretending they liked them, they finished their second cerveza.

A week or so later, they were fortunate enough to meet an older couple who had started for Oregon but decided to return. The boys didn't feel right to question their return but thought they would be helpful with deciding on the necessaries they'd need for the journey. They added to their list: beans, hardtack, dried fruit, more beans, then filled their saddlebags as best they could. The boys then prepared their mounts, carrying fodder if grass got scarce. When wood became scarce, they would use dry buffalo dung for their fires.

Back at the stables Noah shared a story with Jarrett, "Mrs. Pawley told me about how Sourdoughs got their name."

"How's that, Noah."

"Those ol' boys carried some live yeast with them, just a starter, then added some flour and a bit of sugar and they had dough to bake. Always had to keep some yeast so it would grow and repeat, lasted for donkey years, reckon that's the way she told it."

"Wonder if they use sourdough on those wagons goin' West?" Their possibles complete, they left Denver to the cowboys.

"Stay safe boys and remember, keep the Platte on your left and an eye out for them Pawnee."

CHAPTER THREE

The Argonauts headed northwest on their own. Their first destination the North Platte River, a trek of two hundred thirty miles, Jarrett with his 'plains rifle', Noah with his Henry.

"Hey Jarrett, one of those ol' timers said the Platte is too thick to drink and too thin to plow."

"They got that right, Noah. What are you going to name your nag?"

"Thought about calling her after one of those peaks we hiked through on our way to Denver but don't know their names. Just been calling her Shadow, seems to fit."

"How 'bout yours?"

"First, thought about Noah, but that name's already taken. Settled on Crabby, after the sergeant."

"He'd laugh at that."

After reaching the North Platte, the partners had been three weeks following wagon tracks, now mostly traveling west, miles upon miles across prairie and sagebrush desert, ten to fifteen miles a day. Astride their ponies they took a moment looking into the vast, endless distance, feeling small as beings but at the same time large with the suspicion they were part of something special.

"Seems to me we've been crossing an ocean, Noah. Know it's dry but, don't know how to say it, just seems like an ocean."

"Like to see the mountains we're supposed to bump into, gotta be there pretty soon. Be nice to join up with one of those wagons. Bet they can cook better than we can."

"Probably eat more than just rabbits, birds and beans."

"Those prairie hens you're bringing in taste good and you're saving us lead Jarrett, using that slingshot, that's for sure. Where did you learn to do that?"

"When I was little, pa used one to scare off the skunks that were eating our eggs and some hens. That became my job as soon I could shoot straight. Been thinking, you've never shot your Henry except in the back lot of that store. Wonder if we should practice a little."

"Let's do it now", Noah suggested. "Time to stop anyhow, almost eatin' time."

Picking out targets they challenged each other, not exactly marksmen but catching on.

"Look over to your left a little Jarrett, see that wagon wheel? Must've been left by one of the pioneers. Lessee who can make that boy ring." Neither one hit the wheel, but dust flew close.

The travelers had seen furniture, beds and dressers, even a spinet discarded and crude crosses now and then along the road with CHOLERA carved. They felt saddest when seeing a carcass of a noble ox that had died on the trail.

"All those goods deserted, had to be important to carry them all the way from Missouri or Kansas or wherever they came from and then just leave them. Too hard on the animals, even with the folks walking along with their wagons most of the way."

"Is that why you left your books back in San Luis?"

"Yup, too heavy and takes too much space, reckon there's books in California. Thought about hiding a couple in your goods.

Another thing's bothering me, Jarrett. They say those oxen and mules are pulling wagons."

"Correct."

"But the way I see it is they push the wagons."

"How's that, Noah?"

"Well, Jar, they're actually pushing against some kinda' yoke."

Then they heard gunshots.

"Can't be too far away, Jar."

"let's have a look."

Hustling their mounts to an easy canter, they approached carefully.

"I count five of them, Jar, whaddaya' think?"

"Going to be big trouble for that wagon. What say we separate, take them from two sides, make a lotta noise, might scare them off. That makes two apiece and an extra for you. Reckon we'll be a surprise. Sarge tells a story 'bout something like this happened to those trappers up on South Pass."

"You sure can talk a lot Jar, let's go git 'em."

Firing their weapons, the surprised Indians scattered, at least for now. After a spell, the dust cleared and the two horsemen rode to the converted farm wagon.

"Ho", from Jarrett and Noah."

"Ho back to you two. Tie those broncs and I'll check and see if there's any damage.

Howdy, name's Caleb Brewster on my way to the Salt Lake. Looks like you two got here just in time, saved my bacon, thanks. They left quick enough when you two started shooting. Probably young ones feeling their oats. Thanks again."

"Glad to help, Mr. Brewster. This here's Noah and I'm Jarrett Andersen. Noah's my brother. That Salt Lake you mention, would that be the ocean? Me and Noah, we're on our way to California."

"No, that Salt Lake is just that, a big salty lake. The Pacific Ocean is still away off to the west. Jim Bridger told stories about a spot above the lake, about a thousand feet up. Hope to settle there for a while and see what happens. Plenty game and a body should do good."

"You know Jim Bridges, Mr. Brewster?"

"No, just heard some of his tales. Always been a student of those wild men."

"We have a sergeant friend in San Luis, Colorado Territory, that's where we're from. Sarge guided with Mr. Bridger for some time. Name's Crabtree."

"That wouldn't be old Crabby Crabtree, would it?"

"That's our friend, and it's because of him that me and Noah are here now. You know Sergeant Crabtree, Mr. Brewster?"

"No, never fortunate to meet that old soldier, but heard some about him."

The three traded histories for a bit forgetting for a while where they were, pretty much alone.

"Let's vamoose and get clear of this place. Don't want any more of those hellraisers coming back. After all, we're the invaders."

"Never thought of it that way, Mr. Brewster."

"We can talk tonight, after we put some miles between us".

They made a cold camp at dusk.

"No fire tonight, boys. Let's eat cold and keep our hair. I've plenty pemmican."

"Sarge talked about pemmican, said it was Indian food that the trappers learned to use."

"Your sergeant's correct, a mix of venison, dried berries and fat. Pemmican's a Cree word for fat. First thing in the morning while I'm greasing the wheels and fixing the vittles, you might look for decent water. The main stream's mighty muddy."

"Can do that, Mr. Brewster. I'd like to hear more about us being invaders. Thought this was all America, thought President Jefferson bought it for us."

"Depends how you look at this problem, Jarrett. The simple answer is they were here first. The Indian tribes are several sovereign nations"

"What's that sovereign mean, Mr. B?" This from Noah who was becoming more than just a kid from San Luis.

"To me, it means free. The Indian was here first and created his own culture that's different from ours. But still it's their way of life. And we're taking that life from them. Yes, they're warriors, they steal each other's horses and some eat dogs, but it's their way.

Most nations consider themselves superior to all others and most tribal names simply means the People. This is their America and like I said, they were here first a long time ago. Most of us take it away without conscience and I for one are part of their problem"

Noah wondering aloud, "Is it true they keep slaves?"

"Yes, they do. Did your sergeant ever tell stories about Captain Lewis and Captain Clark?"

"Remember Jar, that's what got him to go to the mountains, Lewis and Clark."

"Then he told you about the "Bird Woman."

'That would be Sacagawea, right?"

"Correct, Noah. Sacagawea was a slave, a Shoshone girl kidnapped by Hidatsa when she was twelve. And Captain Clark owned a slave named York, which he never manumitted."

"Got me with that big word."

"Means to set free, Noah."

"Why don't they just say free 'em, reckon those fancy dudes need something to do."

"Jim Beckwourth was a Black Mountain Man, a former slave who was manumitted by his father and master. He trapped for the Rocky

Mountain Fur Company. One day while fixing his traps, he was captured by the Crow. Jim claimed to be a long-lost son of a chief. The Crow not only adopted him they made him war chief of the Dog Clan. Lived with them for nearly ten years. Beckwourth's most famous for telling big stories about himself, certainly exaggerated, especially at rendezvous."

"Speaking of story tellers, Sarge told us Jim Bridger had some woppers. One 'bout fish in a boiling lake. Caught 'em in the cold underneath and when he reeled them in, they were cooked ready to eat."

"We tell lots of stories about the Indian too, and mostly don't know much about them. Lennie Mae, she was like a mom, told me a Bible story once. Some mean men were throwing rocks at a girl who'd done something wrong and Jesus stepped in and said something like, 'Are you so good that maybe she shouldn't throw them rocks back', something like that."

The second night as the small fire was finishing.

"Mr. B?"

"What's that, Noah?

"Just thinking."

"What about, Noah?"

"Couple things, we were talking about slaves and Indians and I got to thinking that white Americans have slaves too, a lot more than the Indian has. Never knew one in San Luis."

"Do you know who sold the slaves that white men bought?"

"Don't know? Who, Mr. B?"

"Africans, Noah. Stronger tribes raided and captured other Africans and sold their captives to white sea captains. Doesn't make it right, but some of the blame must be shared. This problem of slavery just might destroy our country. What else were you thinking about tonight?"

"Just thinking about that big metal spoon you were using to stir the beans."

"What about the spoon?"

"When I was washing up with the beans cleaned off, I was looking. On the outside, I saw my reflection and I was upside down, and on the inside, I was regular, maybe other way around. How come?"

"That's because one is convex and the other concave."

"Sounds a couple fancy words, but I still don't know why?"

"I see you're a thinking man, Noah."

"Reckon I know enough to get out of the rain."

"G'night, Noah," from Jarrett.

After a breakfast of corn bread Johnnycakes, those staples of wagon train pioneers and after greasing the wheels, the three kept west always searching for good water.

"Do you know where we're at, Mr. B.?"

"Not a hundred percent of course, but this scanty map reads we're near South Pass, the easiest to travel by horse or wagon. It's all the land of the aborigine. Like I said, we're the trespassers. It might be a lot safer travelling without a wagon. You boys go on ahead, I should make out."

Jason and Noah both answered, "Nope, they're three of us now, at least till those mountains above that salty lake."

"What's the name of those mountains up ahead, Mr. B?" Noah always keen on learning and remembering names of places.

"Wasatch Mountains first crossed by none other than our friend Mr. Bridger as a young fella. Simply means 'low pass over high range' to the Utes. In Shoshone it means 'blue heron', named after one of their chiefs."

"How come you know so much, Mr. B?"

"I was a teacher, Noah. Taught classes in Indian Studies and the History of Mountain Men at Dickinson College."

"Think if I was going to college, I'd study History, except for all those dates."

"It's a fact Noah, we teachers sometimes dwell on the particulars too much. Always started my classes with, 'Take the hi out of history, and watcha got?'"

"Story?"

"And that's what history is, a story. College got to be too stuffy for me. After reading reports and journals from real Mountain Men, I had to come see for myself. And then history seems to evolve with interpretations and personal biases."

"My problem is I don't know much, can read but still don't know much."

"What's important, Noah, is you're clever and getting a real education out here. Anyway, school can sometimes get in the way of a real education. You, my young friend, are fortunate indeed. Now let's try one of these rabbits Jarrett brought in."

Later after cleaning up and checking on their animals, the three were talking as the fire died. Noah did his best thinking looking at the heavens. "Mr. Brewster, ever wonder about all those stars, must be more than a thousand."

"I do Noah, I do."

"Whadaya think 'bout?"

"I wonder about the Greeks who named all those constellations."

"Heard 'bout them a bit, what about them?"

"As you know Noah, those folks lived a long time ago. They were our mother civilization and believing in only four elements, earth, water, air and fire, shaped a civilization we follow today. See all those different images in the stars, kind of by themselves. Use your imagination. Do you see a pattern of stars that looks like anything you recognize?"

"There's one that looks like an upside-down pitcher."

"Good on you. That one is named the Big Dipper.

And it's not always upside down, depends on the Earth's rotation. There's a smaller one that is named the Little Dipper. And there's Indians with bows and horses and wagons up there. All you have to do is look, Noah, and imagine."

"Do you think if we listen hard enough at night, we might hear those old Mountain Men telling their stories?"

"Maybe just before dawn if there's a hint of a breeze, we might hear the whispers of Meriwether and Sacagawea or most likely Jim Bridger or Beckwourth sharing their tales."

"Thanks Mr. B, goodnight."

"Goodnight boys."

Stopping before noon by a small stream, they shared jerky and filled their water bags, then rested an hour in the scant shade of Caleb's wagon.

Brewster asked, "Last night we were talking about the stars. Ever see a comet?"

Noah replied, "We watched in San Luis, called it the Great March Comet, remember it lasted a long time."

"Excellent. Indians watched as well and are superstitious without the science to explain the phenomena. Back in eleven in the Indiana

Territory, Tecumseh, a Shawnee chief, was federating the tribes getting the nations together to stop the progression of whites. He and a younger brother called The Prophet, a spiritual leader, used the comet to recruit other tribes.

Coincidentally, the Mississippi ran backwards awhile after a series of earthquakes. All this feeds Indian superstition.

Tecumseh and his braves were away from their camp when William Henry Harrison, the Military Governor, attacked the Shawnee village at a place called Tippecanoe burning it to the ground and destroying all their winter's food supply.

Now the interesting part and then we'll leave, Tecumseh allegedly placed a curse on Harrison who in 1840 became our president. Harrison used a slogan 'Tippecanoe and Tyler Too', reminding the folks of his alleged heroism. Tylor was his vice-presidential candidate. President Harrison died thirty-one days after taking office. Tecumseh's curse also includes death for every generation of presidents while holding office, which is about twenty years. Now the road."

The next night, it was Jarrett's turn to pick at Caleb Brewster's brain. "Pardon me for asking Mr. B, but you ever marry?"

"Married once and content." After a pause and a soft sigh, "The cholera got both my wife and two daughters. That's the real reason I decided to look west, get away. Not from their memories but to be by ourselves out here. Can't help feeling guilty. Life's rarely fair. Understand?"

"Reckon so", from both.

They were indeed fortunate, one more week navigating safely. Almost to the Salt Lake.

And the sky seemed bigger than ever.

CHAPTER FOUR

"This coming up must be the Weber river, at least on my scanty map."

Jarrett and Noah felt obliged to Mr. Brewster for the talks they shared since the little skirmish, becoming more of a friend and appreciating him as a mentor.

Three wagons were backed up at the flooded river crossing, waiting for a storm to subside in the high Wasatch. Three Overlander families of pioneers, two in one wagon and four each in the other two were restless after waiting two days reconnoitering.

That evening the professor and the boys were invited to share supper of the usual fare of bread, beans and bacon. More important was the chance to exchange information.

That night after the modest feed with a lot of give and take and some arguing, nothing was decided. Two of the families were patient, one determined to push on right after johnnycakes and coffee.

Back at their close by camp, Jarrett asked, "Professor, what do you think is the better animal for those wagons, oxen or mules?"

"Studied that a bit before I left. Mules are strong and are faster than oxen but can be tricky to handle. Oxen are stronger and very reliable animals and can drag wagons out of mudholes and pull up steep hills. And they'll eat poor grass where a mule is pickier."

Noah asked how much oxen cost.

"A yoke of oxen can cost up to sixty-five dollars and you need three pair for these wagons."

"That makes six oxen for each wagon, they seem to be the real heroes to me."

"And you must protect them from hail and sores from ill-fitting yolks or split hooves. My little wagon is light carrying only my goods and as you know I walk most of the way, as most of these pioneers do. Decided my horse would do for me."

After laying out their bedrolls, the two boys talked things over.

"Dunno what their gonna' do, me, I'd wait. They were talking about Oregon. It'll still be there if they wait another day or two. Seemed they had enough possibles."

"What did you think about those twins in those gingham dresses? Both about as shy as mountain lions, purdysome too."

"Purdysome, that's a new word from you, Noah."

"Means some pretty."

"Well, that purdysome, freckled-faced sister sure fancied you and made a show of letting you know."

"Kinda' skinny. Her ma was pretty though, maybe she'll grow into it."

"Wonder if she's a good kisser, sure seemed to wanna try."

The next morning the wagons struggled lining up, two families still cautious.

"Let's go, I'm tired of wasting time. Been on this trek for three months now."

Two families remained vigilant.

The wagon second in line moved to take the lead fifty yards below the crossing point. Two of the wagons used a team of oxen apiece. The determined family's wagon pulled by six stout mules entered the flow. Almost across, mules, wagon and passengers were swept away by the Weber in flood.

Without two thoughts, Jarrett and Noah urging their mounts plunged in the river. Downstream a mile they found the family struggling in the rapids and pulled them safely ashore on the same side they started. Discouraged and with their wagon in pieces, they were ready to quit. The mules struggled ashore on the far side.

An hour later, the disheveled were back with their companions taking stock of their situation.

"Not much left, come too far to return. This is good land, obviously well-watered. Reckon we'll settle here, up the hill some."

Jarrett and Noah returned pulling a plow, farm tools and some pots and pans they found a little further down river.

"Might find more of your goods when the river slows. There's some boards from your wagon on the shore down there."

"Didn't know anyone could be so nice. But we can't slow you down. We were hard-headed and put everyone in danger."

"Stop this foolishness. Collect them mules and your goods and climb aboard."

And they did.

The next day, Jarrett, Noah and the professor raised their hats to farewell the twins and a God's speed to the families.

"Me and Jarrett's been talking things over professor. Like to ride along a spell, maybe take a look at that Jim Bridger country. Then we'll git on to California, maybe in a couple weeks. We could help you get started."

With merely a hint of a pathway, they rode and pulled the wagon slowly, deeper and higher winding through the forested Wasatch when the arrow hit Caleb deep into his shoulder. Finding cover as best they could, they waited.

"That arrow looks bad, Mr. B. Sarge warned us plenty that this was bound to happen somewhere along the way."

They fired their rifles now and then to remind the Indians they could defend themselves.

"Wonder what Sergeant Crabtree would do?"

"Probably tell them a story," earning a weak laugh.

Then the Indians withdrew.

"What you reckon, Mr. B?"

"Probably a hunting party and not prepared for a long fight. And we have the rifles. Now, cut this arrow out. Which one of you can do it? If Jed Smith can sew back his ear, I can have this taken out. Now get to it while I still have some strength."

With Noah holding the professor down, Jarrett tried cutting the arrow out.

"Don't think I can do this, Noah."

Noah smacked Brewster behind an ear hard enough to knock him senseless.

"Had to do it, Jarrett. Now cut that damn thing out, gotta do it, gotta."

With the professor senseless, the shaft was out.

"He's a tough bird for sure. Didn't know they made teachers like that."

In the morning they checked the professor. Jarrett and Noah were scared, the shoulder looked bad with a black line starting.

"He's real pale Noah, don't know if he can make it. Can't hardly even make him comfortable."

The professor stirred half-awake hot and clammy, mumbling funny.

"He's talking to himself, Jar."

Finally, Brewster came right for a bit and did some self- evaluation.

"It's bad boys, the shaft is out but I can feel the arrowhead. Still lodged in there. Only one thing left to do. Could get blood poisoning, you have to dig deep and dig it out, and quickly. Which one of you has the bark to do it? It's my only chance to see that garden and look down on that big lake."

"I'll do it Noah, sharpen our knifes."

An hour later it was done, both bloody.

"You're a tough ol' bird, Mr. B." It was the only thing Jarrett could think of to say when he came around a half-day later. Noah had started a small fire using his knife and whetstone to spark some dry moss. Cauterizing the wound with a red-hot knife, he next wrapped the shoulder in rags from a dirty shirt. Jarrett and Noah would never forget that sizzle and that smell.

The professor was rambling and mumbling names, barely lucid.

"Caleb, Noah's going back to the road and wait for help, got to be some soon."

"Don't have the time. If I'm to die, I want to go in Bridger's Garden."

Caleb Brewster hung on for two more days.

"Have to bury him Jarrett and make him some kinda remembrance."

"Let's take him in his wagon up to Bridger's garden like he wanted and do it there."

"Good spot right here and there's his lake. Reckon this is Caleb's garden now."

"Got no shovel, how about those rocks over there. We can cover him good, make a memory for him and the critters won't get him."

"Let's leave his wagon and free his horse Noah, kinda be his spirit roaming these Wasatch, and the Indians might find her. Think Caleb would like that."

"Thanks for the lessons, professor."

Collecting Caleb's rifle, ammunition and what useful goods they could haul, they rode back to the trailhead in two days.

"I feel Caleb's going to be just fine, he's with his family now."

"Noah, let's get going and follow that sun." They slowly headed west towards California.

CHAPTER FIVE

"I found her in the Meadow of Broken Trees." I think she is a witch horse. She was once a white man's horse and many white men are witches. She still has one iron foot and the scar that faces with hair put on their horses."

"Then you have touched the horse?"

"No, I have studied her tracks and her print shows one iron hoof."

"Why do you think she's a witch horse, Six Toes?"

"I know because she built a mound of rocks above the Devil Lake that was never there before. There is a white man's house on wheels there too. That must have been her home. I was following her tracks when I found her house.

I came to you Grandmother, because you are one of the wise ones. She is a very pretty horse and doesn't seem to fear me. I would like to have her as my own but do not want the people to be suspicious."

"What you must do Six Toes is seek a vision from the sun. Go find your own private place and pray and fast today and tomorrow. You will know what to do when you return."

He knew where to go to sing his prayers. He climbed a difficult trail to the top of a hill with a commanding view. Six Toes looked into the sun two days and sang his prayers and two nights he suffered the cold.

With reins between his teeth and squeezing tightly with his legs, Six Toes leaned over the side of his pony, his shoulder low on her frothy flank shooting his final arrow true. In the dusty melee, the buffalo somersaulted and went down, three shafts buried deep in her neck. Only then did the boy pause to survey the hunt.

A dozen animals lay slain, the result of a primal and brutal way of life. As the women hurried to do their work of collecting the meat, skin and bones, the hunters were slicing out hunks of liver to celebrate. Six Toes sang a prayer of thanks to the animals that sustained the People.

"Ah, you have returned. It has been, yes, two days. You must be very hungry, but first what have you learned?"

"Grandmother, I am eleven winters and have not your wisdom, but I did feel something. The first day my mind flew like the raven. Then the second noon with the sun the brightest, I saw myself riding the horse on a buffalo hunt, the two of us bringing down animals for the People. The wind spoke to me and I saw the animals as meat, hides to build our homes, winter robes and bones for tools and weapons. I was one with the horse. I have named her Eagle in the Wind because the first day when I lost my way, an eagle was circling and watching me, sending me messages to concentrate. The eagle must be my spirit helper and guardian."

"You have earned some soup and marrow bones, Six Toes. I will speak with your parents and advise them to give you a new name more fitting a young Newe, perhaps Seeks the Truth is a name you would honor. Now after you eat, go and collect Eagle in the Wind."

These Newe as they called themselves or Shoshone meaning the People were the descendants of those Asians who first walked that land bridge across the Bering Strait thirty thousand years ago, spreading to all parts of the Americas, north, central and south, dispersing to form all the various nations and tribes. Because of faulty geography, they were dubbed Indians by the first European visitors.

Away west in California, native people were isolated from social intercourse with other indigenous nations and even from each other because of the rugged topography.

In all three Americas, the wheel was never invented because there were no domesticated beasts to pull or push a device until the arrival of European animals. The Mayan calendar wheel was devised in the fifth century BCE turning minds instead of wheels.

Because of California's gentle climate, there was little need of elaborate housing and an ample food supply aided by a temperate climate contributed to a large population estimated at three hundred thousand when Europeans first arrived.

The People, of course, have their own interpretations of their beginnings.

And then there are some theories that the Chinese might have been the first visitors.

CHAPTER SIX

"Look at all that white, Noah. Nothing but white, a salt desert. Still some faint wagon tracks, somebody got this far. Let's head north and get out of this hell."

Exploring the salty lake for a day, they rode back east a few miles toward the mountains to find good water.

"Sarge said the old trappers held their rendezvous north some days at a Bear Lake, let's find it."

Keeping the Wasatch on their right, they found the lake in five days. Dismounting and after a look around they agreed to take some days to rest and hunt.

"Nice country here Noah, plenty deer sign, stream close by and plenty wood."

After hobbling their horses, setting up camp and building a small fire pit for later, they wandered for a look around. An Indian about their age was sitting on his haunches examining some shards of pottery. He showed neither surprise nor concern when the boys approached.

"This is most interesting. This was made by my people and here it hides, many weeks away from where it was made."

"Howdy. What have you found?"

"Pieces of an old pot made the old way. Maybe brought to the meeting of trappers years ago."

"Do you live close to here?"

"I don't know exactly where I live. I seem to live wherever I end up at the end of a day. My people live in Oregon."

"My brother Noah and I are living the same way. Name's Jarrett, my brother Noah."

"I am called Walks All Trails."

"So, you walk everyplace?"

"Mostly. I collect these treasures when I find them. My sack is getting full, so soon I might return to Oregon and give them to the old ones. Heard some hair on their faces talking about a mountain to the east that looks like a chimney, I would like to see that."

"Come on over to our camp, we'll start a fire and make coffee."

With a small fire going, the coffee was soon ready. They had Caleb's cup for Walks All Trails.

"Where in Oregon did you begin, Walks All Trails?"

"The place I began is called Waiilatpu on the Wala Wala River."

"Is that where you learned to speak good English?"

"Yes. My father had many dreams and saw the future clearly. When I was a small boy, he sent me to the mission school that Mr. Marcus Whitman started. I decided if I stayed, I would become nothing more than a tame Indian. The whites take away what we are and replace it with what we aren't."

The three shared two rabbits that Jarrett brought in. They talked a few hours and slept till dawn.

When Jarrett and Noah woke, they found Walks All Trails gone. Two feathered prayer catchers left as gifts.

Later in the day as they were collecting some firewood, "Look some arrowheads over there, let's keep a few for good luck. Been good to have been at one of those rendezvous Sarge talked about. Can you image?"

"That's about all there is to do nowadays Jar. The good old days are gone, kinda sad."

"Wonder if they'll ever say that about now?"

That night, around the last of the fire, they relaxed, licking venison grease off their fingers. Noah had brought in a small pronghorn antelope that morning.

"You ever think about girls, Jar?"

"Sometimes."

"Ever have a girlfriend in San Luis?"

"Kinda."

"What's that 'kinda' mean."

"Maryalice and me used to kiss, fooling around some, you know."

"No, what's that fooling around mean."

"Come on, Noah."

"Was it tough to leave her behind, Jar?"

"Was, reckon I felt worse than she did. That Stephen Lee guy was always sweet on her. She's probably his girlfriend now."

Always rising before the sun, the two quietly talked as they fixed cold venison.

"I heard them this morning early, Jar."

"Who's that, Noah?"

"The Mountain Men. Didn't see them, just starting to light up, barely heard them. Jim Bridger and Jed Smith talking real soft with Caleb about how he liked the Wasatch. And an Indian boy was riding Caleb's horse. Then I kinda dozed again and they were gone."

The boys had left San Luis late March with two months in Denver, then the road and the wagon-crossing incident and some time with the professor.

"The days are long, Noah, what month you reckon it is?"

"Been working on that Jar, probably July, maybe August. California will still be there for a while."

"Just chewing on it myself, thinking about winter. Looks like we have maybe two months, before the snow."

"What snow is that?"

"Sarge talked 'bout those California mountains, called them the Sierra, some Spanish name. Anyway, he said they were mighty and not to be taken lightly. They had to be gotten over before winter."

"Plenty to chew on all right. Those Wasatch were nothing to fool with. If your Sierra are anything more, we gotta be smart. How long to reach these Sierra?"

"Reckon a piece, at least."

"That far, eh?"

"Since there's nobody to ask, let's go find them ourselves. Should be some wagon ruts pretty soon, that'll be our map."

They found their trail a bit north and mostly west and in two weeks, Fort Hall.

"Howdy, men. Looks like you've come a bit. Were ya from?"

"San Luis, Colorado Territory, Name's Andersen, both of us. where are we?"

"Reinbolt's my name, call me Richard. Why, you're now at Fort Hall. This is the decision point."

"What decision is that?"

"Whether to head for California or for Oregon. The smart ones choose Oregon. The few, foolish enough or brave enough head west to California. Me, this is where I decided to stay with my family. Nice little trading post here and the Bannock and Shoshone are mostly friendly, just gotta watch your possibles. Which trail you gonna elect?"

"Reckon we'll elect for California. Think we'll stick around a while, maybe a week or so, need information and lot of advice."

"Tell ya what, my place is only three miles directly north on a darn good track. When you're ready, ride on up. Wife always has a roast goin' and room at the table for two more. Nice section of the Snake River close by where you can camp. Be nice to talk and we'll tell ya all we know about the California Trail. The kids would 'preciate the company too. Truth is, it's a little lonely for the young ones."

Jarrett and Noah spent three days with the Reinbolt family gleaning all they could about the way to California.

"It's going to take some time to get ourselves to California Jar, maybe we could do some chores around the fort, hunt for the folks and trade for some of the goods we need."

"Let's take some venison up to Richard. He can hunt right outside his door but be nice to say thanks and think he would like the chance to git his fiddle goin' again."

Exploring the fort established in 1834 as a fur trading post and escaping a second day of drizzle, they found two friends, the twins. The family had quit their trek close to Fort Hall. The girls were pleased to be finished with the hard wagon trail life. And, they already had a boyfriend on their arms.

"That sure was a quick romance there Noah, just a hello before we find out about their new love lives."

"Womenfolk are scarce out here Jar, not enough to go around, especially the unmarried purdysomes. So far it's mostly a country for men."

"Seeing those folks at the fort made me think about the Arnolds' back home, they'll always stay special with me, Noah. Reckon you're my family now."

"Maybe there's ladies waiting for us in California."

"Let's go find them, Jar."

They recharged for two weeks collecting all the particulars they

needed. Hunting plentiful mule deer, they traded venison for sugar
at the fort, then swapped the sugar with the Shoshone for pemmican.
Richard had given them each a parfleche, those rawhide, envelope-
shaped containers which were perfect for carrying their pemmican.
And they carried extra fodder for the horses.

CHAPTER SEVEN

Seven hundred dry miles to reach Sutter's Fort.

"Richard sure was frontier friendly and knew some about California. Shared what he heard from the guides and soldiers that travel the trail. Interesting about this Sutter guy who started his settlement. Some sort of foreigner and some kinda king or something. Sounds like he owns California. This little adventure of yours is getting good, Jar."

"And all that talk about that Death Desert. Gotta miss that and then Sergeant Crabtree's Sierra. One hoof and one moccasin after the other. The fort folks said it was September and that's good news."

After topping their water bags, they found the desert in two-weeks. The dry was intimidating but it wasn't a killer, at least not his year. The days were hot and the nights were cold. Starting with dawn, they rode a mile and they walked two miles, over and over, sucking small stones to slack their thirst. When they did sip water is was hot, but it was wet. Resting during the heat of the day, they would then continue till dusk. At the end of each day their faces above their bandanas and below their hats were dark from the sun and the dust of the desert. Their camps were always dusty, waterless and without shelter. Unwilling to eat sagebrush, their horses ate short grasses to survive and found seeps to drink from.

"What year is this, Jar?"

"Reckon it's 1847, Noah."

Noah wondered aloud as they took their midday feed. "Jar, why do most all folks look different and dogs mostly too when deer and squirrels and toads all look the same?"

Jarrett was used to and enjoyed these queries, but this one stumped him.

Jarrett countered, "I miss the cookies, Noah?"

"What cookies are that, Jar?"

"Lennie Mae's, full of nuts and molasses."

"Now I'll stay awake all night."

"Why would that be?"

"Thinking of cookies full of nuts and molasses."

"I'll probably stay awake thinking of all those scorpions and rattlers that are living with us."

This night, their horses seemed apprehensive maybe sensing something. They made a cold camp.

"Miss the fire Noah, got a funny feeling. Remember Sarge talking about trusting yourself. I'll sit a bit, get some sleep my brother."

Morning arrived without incident. "How's our animals?"

"Calm Noah, nice and calm. Curious last night, I felt something. Maybe this desert has ghosts. Let's keep our eyes open and watch behind us as well as ahead. Keep our rifles clean and oiled."

The trouble came at midday.

"Hardly a breeze so far, Jarrett. But there's dust on your left, just beyond those low red hills, don't think it belongs there, just a funny feeling again."

"Let's hold up. Not much cover around here. Might be some trouble of some sort. Hundred yards ahead might give a little shelter."

"We can check things out from there. Got that feeling myself."

From their scant hide they hobbled their horses. With rifle's ready they waited. An hour's wait with the sun directly in their eyes, the attack came.

"Hard to tell for sure but it seems to be five of them."

"That means there's two for me and three for you, Noah."

In the first attack, Jarrett and Noah each brought down a raider. The remaining bandits retreated to reconnect.

"Wonder who these boys are? Don't look like Indians, bandits most likely."

"Gonna wait us out, pard. Can do without food for a couple days, water's the hitch. Us and the horses but they might be in the same pinch. Can't wait much longer."

"What's the plan, Jarrett?"

"They'll wait till dark and then come for us. Let's beat them to it, go get them now, you on the right and me on the left. Won't expect us during the hot. Three of them left, two for you, amigo and one for me."

"Okay, nice and easy, pretend you're one of the professor's braves, nice and easy."

With shadows on the long side, they quietly snaked then rushed the gunmen. Jarrett nailed one, Noah the others.

"Don't look very successful bandits. Reckon they were desperate. Kinda feel sorry for them. Can't dig in this stuff, let's bury them under all these rocks."

And the dust devils danced.

CHAPTER EIGHT

Without knowing, they crossed into California two weeks later, soon to be eighteen.

"Been thinking Jar."

"Don't wear yourself out, Noah."

"When we do get to California, how do we know we're there? Is there a welcome sign? Some of those folks might have a band and some speeches for you. Maybe that king guy they were talking about back at Fort Hall. You figured what we're gonna do when we git to wherever we're gittin'?"

"Have a bit."

"Well Jar, what you figured?"

"There's only one thing we can do."

"And what might that be?"

"I used to be a cowboy when I was young."

"And now that you're old?"

"Maybe the king could use a couple cowboys."

"Appreciate you considering me Jar."

"Pleasure Noah."

A mirage a few days and then slowly a hint and in a few days more a massive delight. "Reckon those are Sergeant Crabtree's Sierra ahead."

"How do we get over those boys? Looks to be mighty steep and high."

"Let's find out."

Following Indian trails through canyons that followed animal trails following streams, climbing, always climbing they found their way.

'What's that word Caleb used when talking 'bout those Wasatch, when we were climbing the steep part?"

"Perpendicular?"

"Yup, that's the word. Perpendicular."

"How come you thought of that word Noah?"

"These mountains are more perpendicular than them Wasatch perpendiculars and those wiggly yellow trees remind me of San Luis."

"You could do a lot of whittling here."

And then a majesty of blue.

"There's a sight that makes this all worthwhile, Noah."

"Never seen anything like that lake, Jarrett."

"Glad there's no folks to spoil."

"Be interesting to be the first soul out here and then you could name everything as it came along. I'd call that big peak yonder, Mt. Noah."

"That blue lake makes me think of women."

"Women?"

"Yup."

"How's that?"

"Dunno, kinda' calm right now but maybe with a big wind, might get wild."

"Keep thinking on it, Noah."

Snowed steady that night and three days and nights more, sleeping impossible with only scant remains of jerky to chew and little fodder for their horses. The trail disappeared. Struggling by trial and error, they crossed the divide, the western side gentler. Finally, in three hungry days out of the heavy snow, they stopped and built a small fire. Jarrett trapped two trout and they feasted. Their horses found grasses under the snow.

"There's a wagon trail, Jar, must be getting' close."

"To where?"

"To the castle of course."

"Of course."

For a week they followed a river which settled on a lovely valley. Fat trout kept them fed.

"Getting crowded, counted near to fifty folks so far. This must be your California. Don't see an ocean, though. Let's jump in that river and wash ourselves, even our clothes." It was icy-cold, but the sun warmed them and finally dried their garb. "Think you need to look nice for the king. Maybe they'll be a princess, maybe two."

"You don't have much of a beard to wash Jar."

"You neither Noah, just a little fuzz. Don't even know what I look like. Wonder if I would recognize myself?"

"Why don't we change names? Then we could recall each other."

"Huh?"

It would take a few baths more to get that gritty, jealous desert out of their skin.

Jarrett and Noah were confused. The king was just a man. John Augustus Sutter, a pioneer born in Germany used both Mexican and American citizenship. And he was neither and California wasn't even Mexico or America! California was California, coveted by America, recently lost by Mexico. And Sutter named his colony New Helvetia, a Latin name for Switzerland. His fort was a small stockade without a princess.

Jarrett and Noah needed work.

"Disappointed, Jar."

"Why's that, Noah?'

"First there's no band at the border, wherever that was and then expected a king and a castle and princesses. The castle's nothing but a couple of small buildings. And the Indians around here sure don't look happy, look abused. Wonder what their story is? Let's move on Jar, what next for us?"

"Let's try some of these ranchos."

The third they tried, two hour's east and south of Sutter's offered them work.

"Being from San Luis helps, we can speak a little Spanish, Jar. How we gonna' work this? Maybe this Señor Nieto we heard about talks some American." And he did.

"Cannot pay pesos, but camas to sleep. You like Mexican comida?"

"Bueno with me, how 'bout you, Noah?"

"Bueno, Señor Nieto y gracias."

The new vaqueros found worn boots that almost fit in the bunkhouse to replace their ragged moccasins.

The rancho, measured in square miles, was once a Spanish land grant seemingly without boundaries, with cattle on a hundred hills. Animals weren't harvested for food. Fat was rendered to make tallow and shipped to light the world along with the hides for leather. Of course, enough roasts and steaks survived for barbecue. The New

Year's celebration was Mexican style with a fiesta. They toasted 1848 with tequila.

"Never had it so good Jarrett. Like your California. No work tomorrow, let's head up those hills and have a look. Make a fishing pole and try our luck. Lots of snow this winter, should make the river full."

"Practicing my Spanish with the vaqueros. They call it the American River, supposed to have some nice trout. Wonder if the fishing's as good as Colorado."

"Learning more Spanish every day myself, talking with the vaqueros, seems if you try, they're ready to help, all you have to do is try."

"What do you talk about, Jar?"

"Why this isn't even Mexico like we thought. Had a revolution a while back and now they own their own country, call themselves the Bear Republic with their own flag and everything, picture of a grizzly on it. They joke that the bear looks like a pig.

Things are changing with Anglos settling around here lately and nobody's happy with any of the bosses. Don't want to be Mexican or Americanos. Want to be Californios, be their own boss. Then there's some American soldiers nosing around stirring folks up."

Captain John C. Freemont on a third 'scientific' expedition had been in and out of California for three years, an invader. Relations between Mexico and the United States were tenuous. President James Polk had given instructions to be alert in case war broke out between the two nations. Fremont, the 'Pathfinder', and his sixty soldiers were ready. The soldiers had problems with the Indians, killing several along the trail and finally punishing the Klamath, destroying an entire village in retaliation after they had killed three of Freemont's party.

On April 25, 1846, war was declared between Mexico and the United States, ending February,1848.

June and July of 1846, the short-lived Bear Flag Republic and on January 24, 1848, gold was discovered on Sutter Creek, near Colima by James Marshall and changed the world.

Nearly three hundred thousand 49ers mortgaged their property, borrowed money or spent their life savings to travel overland to California, or by sea from the East and Europe. Some sailed to

Panama and hiked that arduous trail across to the Pacific side and then another ship to San Francisco. Others chanced the route around Cape Horn only to find they needed another one hundred fifty miles to the gold fields. They came from South America, New Zealand and Australia. They left their women to run the businesses or to farm, raising children alone. Some took as long as nine months for the journey. All for the dream of wealth.

After nearly two years, of war, President Polk's prize was the Southwest, especially California with her gold and a lot more. The Treaty of Guadalupe Hidalgo ceded what would become New Mexico, Utah, Nevada, Arizona and western Colorado, all for fifteen million dollars to the United States.

Polk was ready to take on the British as well. His 1844 election slogan, 'Fifty-Four Forty or Fight' referring to lines of latitude separating the United States and Canada, led to his victory against all odds.

"Reckon we're back to being Americans again, Noah."

"Yup, for all of us, Indian, Mexican and Anglos."

"Hope we all remember that."

"Do like this buena vida rancho life Noah and there's some pretty señoritas over in the villages but I got an itch again."

"Oro becha', heard some stories. Wouldn't mind having a looksee myself. Hate to leave our jefe but let's at least give it a try."

Five weeks after the new year they talked with Señor Nieto who understood, giving each an old dishpan and one rusty shovel. He told them he thought big dinero would be made selling goods to folks who were bound to try the streams. Senor Nieto was content with his riches, family and rancho.

They rode their horses to the foothills where the oaks met the pines. Before the changes, Californios rarely used cash, preferring a barter system. It was rumored that Catalina, an island down south was traded for a silver-studded saddle.

"Good thing we got here first, Noah. These streams are gonna get busy when the news gets to the cities. Folks might even come as far as San Luis. Be special to find Sarge at the end of a shovel."

They had no clue what to do. Sitting on their haunches they studied the moving water and thought.

"What do you reckon, Jarrett?"

"Dunno exactly, just watching the flow. The only gold I ever held was that twenty-dollar piece back in Colorado. Kinda heavy. Gold must be a kinda rock."

"I see where you're going with this. Heavy stuff rolls with the current, might settle in the calm sides of the river as it makes its turns. Gotta start someplace, let's try."

A week they tried this theory.

"Well Noah, reckon I'm not a miner, just a vaquero and that's not bad. Tired of bending over in this ice water that was snow yesterday. Besides, nothing but trout. Good you made a fishing pole or we'd be hungry *and* poor. Keep thinking of comida, señoritas and cervezas. Ready to head home when you are."

"Okay with me Jar, let's pan that other side three days. Then go help Señor Nieto with his cows."

CHAPTER NINE

"Jarrett, some color here." Swirling his pan slowly, the lighter sand washed away leaving a heaver type. "It's kinda glinty, is it gold?"

"Reckon it's gold, amigo."

A week later around their fire, they evaluated their options.

"How much you need, Noah?"

"Enough for a good place to live, a good horse and friends. And that's what I got before this gold. Don't need two houses or two horses. Already have a best amigo and a brother."

Two weeks of digging and swirling and mostly failing, they decided they had enough.

"How much we got, Jar?"

"Near a pound."

"How much is that?"

"Dollars or pesos?"

"Dollars."

"More than enough."

"That much?"

"Noah let's give it another week and get back to la buena vida. Some characters are starting to show on the river."

Later that very day, "Howdy, how's it going?" From an Anglo, not dressed for prospecting.

Jarrett answered vaguely, "Howdy, lookin' for gold, gotta be here someplace on the river. We've been workin' a few weeks now and no color yet. But we're not givin' up."

"So, you haven't staked any claims yet?"

"Nope. Like I said we're not givin' up. My pard and I gonna keep tryin' for a few more days and then we'll look for another stream. Hear the Bear River's runnin' rich, might try up there next."

The suspicious stranger mounted and rode down river.

"Who's that, Jarrett?"

"Dunno, but I don't trust him, something greasy about that hombre."

A gracias to the river and they returned to the rancho, their prospecting days history. Things were different when they arrived. Señor Nieto was gone. An Anglo met them as they entered the property.

"Howdy boys, what's your business?"

"Our business isn't your business. Where's Señor Nieto and all the vaqueros?"

"But it is our business, since this is our ranch."

"Must have hearing problems Jarrett. Did he say his ranch?"

"You heard right fellas and if you don't have business here, on your way pronto unless you want to cowboy for Mr. Bedford."

"Don't know nothing' 'bout a Mr. Bedford. Where's Señor Nieto?"

"Probably Sacramento crying to the court. Fat chance. Mr. Bedford owns the ranch now and the bank and the sheriff."

"Okay, my pard and I will collect our goods and leave just as you suggest."

"You got no goods. Everything belongs to Mr. Bedford."

"Then how about that job?"

"Changed my mind, don't need no help after all. Adios."

The two ex-cowboys and ex-prospectors left.

"What's all that and why did you play the fool, Jar. I know you, must have some kinda idea."

"I do Noah,"

And he did.

Jarrett strategized with Noah, as they rode a long day to Colima, a village close to where Marshall found his gold. Finding a cantina was easy, earning trust of the Mexicans was near impossible.

Taking a table in the back, they debated Jarrett's plan.

"Jarrett, how do we convince them we're straight?"

"Gotta use all the Spanish we have."

Jarrett tried talking with a reluctant vaquero he recognized from Señor Nieto's rancho.

After a quiet conference in a corner of El Gitano, one of the more intimidating Mexicans approached. In a mixture of Spanish and English he asked for more particulars. Jarrett detailed his plan and asked for his ideas to get Señor Nieto's rancho back. A few of the vaqueros must have vouched for the Americanos.

"¿Cuando nos vamos?"

"Midnight."

Six rode back to the hacienda.

"Hard to surround the place with half-dozen hombres, Jar."

"Before they get all their cowboy banditos here, we'll give them a surprise. Lucky to find those miners and they let loose of a little dynamite. Didn't cost anything either, just directions to our river and we're through with it."

"It's their river now and good luck to them."

There were no guards and the vaqueros made good sneaks. First, they secreted the horses from the sleeping trespassers. Next, they placed the explosives strategically. In the wee hour before dawn, Jarrett lit the fuses.

Nine smoky, confused and wounded raiders stumbled and collapsed outside. Surveying the damage, they found no harm to the hacienda, the bunkhouse destroyed. The main casa was empty, saved for the mysterious Mr. Bedford. Three bruised mujeres staggered from the ruins.

Speaking rapidly, the women explained to the vaqueros who then translated to Jarrett and Noah.

"They were raped mucho tiempos, kept as slaves by tres hombres malos."

"What three?"

The women identified the three.

"The vaqueros want to hang them, Jar. Too good for them is the way I reckon."

They hanged them, all three.

"Keep them up there as a warning."

Collecting their mounts, they rode back to El Gitano. Jarrett counseled caution.

"They'll come back, back with their friends. No celebrar todivar."

Buying a jug of mescal, they retreated to a hideout in the foothills, now compadres as well as vigilantes.

That night, Noah asked Jarrett what he thought about the hanging.

"First time I killed somebody that wasn't trying to kill me, Noah.

Did shoot at that bunch that killed Caleb, didn't kill anybody. Don't like it much. Then those bandits in the desert. No, don't like it."

"The vaqueros say there's talk in the pueblos calling us banditos and worse."

"That's the Anglos, the Californios have gentler names for us like Los Vigilantes. Do you think we can win?"

"Nope, don't. But we made a statement, Jar. Maybe some quality folk will listen, maybe some of those folks in Sacramento and San Jose and Monterrey. That's all we can hope for, now we gotta disappear. Should be easier for the Mexicans to blend in. Hopefully, Señor Nieto will get his rancho back."

Riding quietly back through the outskirts of the rancho, nothing had changed with other Anglos on patrol.

"Seems the same, Jar. At least we got our rifles and kits back from the raid. We made some enemies, but we made some friends with the Mexicans. Let's go find out a little about Mr. Bedford."

Entering Sacramento, they looked around for a week, spending a little of their gold on digs, tortillas, chiles and frijoles.

"Can't do it. No justice here, Bedford's too well protected, never even leaves his house. It's important but we can't win this one, he's too damn powerful. Let's remember but leave."

"Where to Jar?"

"Heard a little about that Yerba Buena place, good as any other. Let's go and the ocean's close."

About three hundred slaves were brought to the gold fields followed by free African Americans. When California joined the United States as a free state, the 1850 census listed nine hundred sixty-two black residents, many former slaves gaining freedom. However, because of government neglect, slavery flourished within California's 'free' borders. In 1852, a state fugitive slave law made it illegal for slaves to leave their master.

Even so, African Americans continued to move West and in 1852, they numbered two thousand, one percent of the population. These free Americans were barred from testifying in court or sending their children to public schools. With the passage of the Fifteenth Amendment in 1870, the African American won the right to vote. California was Anti-Slavery but not Anti-Racist.

Peter Burnett, California's first elected governor, was a former slave holder from Tennessee who led unsuccessful legislation banning blacks from the state. He signed the Act for the Government and Protection of Indians which enabled whites to force native people from their land into indentured servitude. Burnett's vision of white exclusiveness fit in with attitudes of the time. As a state Supreme Court Justice, he supported a fugitive slave law which was in violation of California's constitution.

In the presidential election of 1860 nearly twice as many Californians voted Democratic as voted Republican, but the Democratic votes were split between John Breckinridge and Stephen Douglass. Republicans were solidly behind one candidate. California's four electoral votes went to Illinois congressman Abraham Lincoln and his running mate, Hannibal Hamlin.

CHAPTER TEN

Boarding the stern-wheeler *Sitka* with the horses stowed below decks, they steamed slowly through the sloughs and narrow channels. They arrived with more than what they started with in San Luis. They both had their rifles and the gold, Jarrett his slingshot.

At the end of 1848, sleepy shantytown Yerba Buena of a thousand had evolved into San Francisco and had grown to nearly twenty-five thousand vibrant souls. The Barbary Coast was born in those wild western days, supporting violence and vice. San Francisco's overwhelmed with the desperate and bold, criminals and politicians, the stew of corruption.

Jarrett and Noah reckoned they were close to nineteen years. A lot of life packed into less than two decades.

"In all my time Noah, never seen this many people added together. The Denver rodeo was the biggest bunch I ever saw at one time."

"What are we going do with our horses, Jar? We could board them out of town. This place makes me uneasy. Too loud and busy for a kid from San Luis."

They found a stable just east of town and rode a public carriage to Chinatown, where they changed their gold to paper, keeping a few smaller nuggets apiece.

"Let's see this place and vamoose, ride south along the coast and have a look at Monterrey. Still a lot of ranchos and we can cowboy when we need to."

"Our stash of dollars oughta last some time."

"Whoa, what the hell was that, Noah?"

"Dunno, never felt anything like it, ground was swaying and shaking for a minute there. Like getting drunk without drinking."

"Must be one of those earthquakes Caleb told us about making the Mississippi go backwards. If I didn't know, I'd think like an Indian being I'm a little superstitious myself."

"Heard this place is called the City of Seven Hills. Wouldn't want one of those coming down on us."

Hailing another horse-carriage, they sightsaw and discovered a wharf with fishing boats and tried crab and shrimp in one of the several restaurants along the wharf.

"Never tasted comida like this, amigo."

"Me neither Noah, might make this a habit if we were staying."

"Too many hills for me, Jar."

"Why Noah, you're from high up in San Luis. You never complained before, and you didn't seem to mind the professor's Wasatch or the Sergeant's Sierra."

"Nope, but there was no shaking and a lot of space in between."

Then on a whim, they rode out of town north to Sonoma and toured the last and most northern Spanish mission with barracks for soldados to discourage the Russian advance.

Chaparral and oaks trees, a few vineyards on hills, Sonoma, a land waiting.

Fort Ross was a Russian outpost in California reaching south from Alaska. Established in 1812 near Bodega Bay, the colony included a sealing station on the Farallon Islands off San Francisco. The fort had a population of twenty-six Russians who maintained the fort until 1841. The main purpose of the fort was the hunting of sea otters for their fur.

"This Sonoma's a place I like better than San Luis or Bridger's Garden, Noah. Here I could settle."

"Tell you what Jar, let's go back south down to Monterrey like we talked about, have a look, then ride back here. They must need cowboys and we sure got the time and the means."

On the road south, they stopped for the night in San Francisco. The boys becoming men decided to have a hoot and found the Barbary Coast, vile with debauching dives and opium dens. Chancing on what looked like one of the nicest taverns, The Escape, they entered through swinging doors. Painted women grabbed them and led them to the bar.

"Watcha' drinkin', handsome?"

"I'll try one of those beers coming out of that spout there, okay with you, Noah?"

"Two Boca Lagers and a lady's drink for me Calico, if that's okay. You seem the generous type." Before he could answer, the drinks slid down the bar.

Joined by another gal, their new lady friends suggested a table in a corner. After two beers from California's first brewery, they felt dizzy.

"Feelin' kinda funny, Jar."

"As well."

"Nothin' like a good shot of whiskey fellas to cure what ails ya."

And it did. Put them right to sleep. "What easy suckers these two are. Get Calico Jim, he knows what to do."

CHAPTER ELEVEN

When he woke, he hurt!

"Jar you there?" Noah felt like he'd been kicked in his stomach. "Jar where are you, amigo?" It was quiet except for some different noises, some creaks and then a kind of a low moan. He was in some dark room on a damp wooden floor, his head not improving.

"Is that you Noah?"

"Think so."

"What the hell, where are we? Feels kinda like Mr. B's wagon. Hurts my head to talk, think I'll try and sleep a little more. Guess this is what they call a hangover."

"Think it's worse than that, Jar."

"Thought you might say something like that."

An hour later they found out where they were.

"Looks like we got lucky with couple a big, strong lads to help us rig some sail, Alf. Waddaya think?"

"Look good to me, better get the cap."

"What's going on?" We in jail?"

"Probably wish you were."

"Don't remember much, don't think we got in any trouble last night. Noah?"

"Nope."

"Come on topside and have a look, that'll answer your first question."

And it did.

"We're on some kinda' boat, Jar."

"That you are, and you'll be aboard for a while."

"Where's San Francisco?"

"Gor, that's a good one. Captain, meet the new crew."

"First, let me set things straight. You've been what they call shanghaied. A mean trick's been played on you. We need men to run this vessel. Most of our sailors jumped ship for the streams and the gold. It's that simple, your sailors now at least till we make port in Canton."

"What's Canton?"

"Not what, but where?"

"Okay, where's Canton?"

"China. Now you have two choices: Cooperate, do your jobs and in a month, you can get off this bucket. Look at it this way fellas, a free tour to Asia."

"Another good one, Cap."

"Well, what say you, easy or hard?"

"We don't know anything about boats Captain, we're from San Luis. That's Colorado Territory."

"Couple bright boys like we got here oughta learn fast if they wanna eat, Cap."

"Might as well make the best of it, Jar."

And they did.

Jarret and Noah became sailors. All new: floors were decks, walls-bulkheads, stairs-ladders, ceilings-overhead, kitchen-galley, windows-portholes, doors-hatches. They learned to climb a mast barefoot to furl and unfurl sails with dramatic sunrises and sunsets. It wasn't all romantic, they scrubbed decks and cleaned heads and the food was lousy.

"Not bad Jar, but the only meat is this salt pork and these weevils in the biscuits for a little flavor." The *Shirley Mae* with one mast and squared-rigged was a twenty-five-meter sloop. It sported a fore-and-aft mainsail with jib, needing a crew of ten. They had eight, their mates were in the California diggings.

The dawns and the dusks were magnificent and the days mostly peaceful. At night the constellations were competing with the heavens of the Oregon Trail, skies that never end.

Later in their third week, finished with their watch with a day turning sour, they were resting in their hammocks. "HIT THE DECKS LADS, WE GOT WEATHER!"

Jarrett was climbing the mast, checking the rigging. Resting a moment on the boom to survey, he found a tangle with the downhaul and the jib halyard.

Shouting into the wind and rain, "N O A H!" Again, "N O A H! Found a problem. Need help, slide to your starboard, there's a tangle."

"Can't hear ya'."

"DOWNHAUL, DOWNHAUL AND JIB!"

"Got it!"

And he did.

Two days and nights to fight the tempest.

"This isn't a British man o' war men but it's the best I can do, here's a tot of rum we carry for strictly medicinal uses."

The sailors coughed, appreciating the captain's generosity.

"That was a bad blow and with only a partial crew. Well done, mates."

The *Shirley Mae* reached China in thirty-one days. Jarrett and Noah rich with another experience. What now? The day before landing, they requested a meet with Captain Hartman.

"Thanks again men, a fine job. You could have been a problem. I was desperate with my sailors deserting for the gold fields."

"Ugh Captain, did you find anything of ours, when we were carried aboard?"

"No, did not. Why do you ask?"

"We had money captain, considerable!"

"Those bastards, probably Calico Jim. They have a team of rascals, from what I hear. They gave you a Mickey."

"What's a Mickey?"

"A Mickey Finn is a drugged drink they sneaked on you."

"Let's meet ashore, I'd like to hear a bit of your history. It'll take me a half-day to finish here. Here's some coin, go find Mao Mao Chung's. It's a fairly decent restaurant but watch each other's backs."

The rickshaw man found Mao Mao Chung's in ten minutes, navigating crooked and crowded lanes with more bicycles than pedestrians, folks hurrying to and from destinations.

"How much we got, Jar?"

"Let's see, all silver coins, looks like about twenty dollars."

"That's what we started with from Denver."

"You're a born philosopher, Noah."

They were cautious and waited for Captain Hartman to arrive before ordering food.

"There you are. Cleared customs and all's good."

"What was our cargo, Captain?"

"Let me get a beer first, then I'll fill all the holes. The Chinese have been brewing beer for seven thousand years and know the trade. Drink up."

"Got a few questions about the *Shirley Mae*. What cargo were we delivering? Will you sail with goods back to Frisco?"

"Can you find a crew here in Canton?"

"What do you think we carried, Noah?"

After a careful sip, "Some hides and tallow, not much else in California that I saw."

"Correct, China has few cattle to speak of, plenty water buffalo but they're farm animals and used for hauling. Chinese have no hankering for beef. They work the hides and use tallow for lighting. What might surprise you, we carried one hold full of laundry. Seems it's quicker and cheaper than waiting in The City to have it done. Then we return with the clean. Chinese know how to wash and press whatever has to be done quick and cheap. Don't know how they do it, but they keep it all organized so the proper folks get theirs back. There's talk that ships might be hauling coolies, Chinese labor to work the new mines and there's rumors about building a railroad back east. As far as crew, that was done after I cleared customs today. Happens to be six Dutch sailors stranded and I hired them all. Their ship's in dry dock for a major overhaul, seems they got hit hard in a typhoon."

"Lucky for you, Captain Hartman. What's a typhoon?"

"Big storm Jarrett, twice as bad as what hit us. You might have heard of a hurricane. Exactly the same, a typhoon is a hurricane on the west side of the International Date Line. They're called cyclones in the Indian Ocean."

Another beer, another question.

"One more thing I'm curious about, what's a clipper? Heard the word tossed around Frisco and wondered what it meant."

"A Clipper is a three-mast schooner, fast, real fast. Big competition between the captains to see who can clip time off the previous record. Big prize money. Thought about what you two will do next? I can always find room for two good sailors."

"Thanks Captain Hartman, we've chewed it over a bit about what we're gonna to do and decided to hang around Canton, see if we can get into some trouble. There's lots of activity in the port. When we're ready to leave, think we might get a ride back working a ship."

"That will work but they'll be no jobs in the port itself. Chinese work for pennies."

"How soon do you leave, Captain Hartman?"

"Three days. Think smart, boys."

They would consider it.

CHAPTER TWELVE

Back to Mao Mao Chung's the next day to talk things over and make a plan during dishes of rice, vegetables and pork. If one didn't know the lingo, one had to point out things and take a chance.

"This is really good Noah, wonder what it's called. Smells good too."

"Interesting little hotel we're staying in Jarrett, a little basic even for us. Where we gonna go from here?"

"Have most of the twenty dollars left. From the prices of rickshaws and beers and the feed we just had, it should last awhile."

"How far is awhile, Jar?"

"Maybe a month."

"There's a fellow in the corner looks kinda like us, maybe American."

Just then, their eyes locked and a slight nod from the stranger.

Half-hour later two beers arrived.

"Sorry mate, but we didn't order these."

The waiter nodded towards the corner and the corner nodded back to their table.

As they were finishing the beers, the stranger approached their table. With a bow and a touch of his cap, the fair tall man, maybe fifty, introduced himself. "Meneers, my name is Van Djik. May I sit a moment?"

"Sit please, and thanks for the beers. Sorry I can't quite wrap around that name."

"Van Djik, please call me Johannes. Let's have one more and I will make clear my interest in you two men."

"I'm Jarrett, this here's Noah."

"Are you a builder of ships, Noah?"

Noah recognized the tired humor with a smile. As they drank their beer and one more, Van Djick told his story."

"I represent a company in The Netherlands. You might know us as Dutch. I am rather like a banker. Do you know the tulip, Meneers?"

"Can't say I do. You, Noah?"

"Nope, what's a tulip Johannes?"

"It is a flower, quite lovely."

"We're from San Luis, that's in Colorado Territory, don't think we grow tulips there. Where's The Netherlands, Johannes?"

"Europe, Noah."

"Near them Greece people maybe?"

"In a way, yes."

"What way is that, Johannes?"

"Several days away by carriage or ship."

That seemed to momentarily satisfy, Noah.

Meneer Van Djick explained the tulip trade: "Tulipmania has captured the world market with some bulbs valued sometimes six times the average of an annual salary. The Age of Reason still challenges traditional thought and much of this thinking still influences the nineteen-hundreds. Tulips are an international exchange of value."

"Does that mean that flower bulbs have taken the place of money?"

"Not entirely, but yes Jarrett, some bulbs are worth more than gold. I have a misfortune and require help. My secretary and administrator is off to San Francisco in three days, he cannot resist the lure of gold. Frankly, I have been deserted."

"Just wondering Johannes, do all you folks in The Netherlands speak American?"

"Most do Noah, but our national language is Dutch."

"Well you sure speak good." Noah enjoyed his game of being a little slow.

"If we could meet again Meneers, I would like to discuss a possible proposition for you. Would you meet me in my office tomorrow, maybe ten? It is close to the docks and easy to find. Look for the sign that reads "DE JONGS LTD. Rickshaw drivers all know the way."

"We can do that, Johannes. Thanks for the beers."

The next day, Noah had the same question he asked on the Platte, this time about the rickshaws. "Jar, are they pulling or pushing?"

They noticed the obvious poverty the closer the docks, folks living wretched, smells mixed between sweet rotten and sour cabbage.

Arriving a bit early, they pulled the bell. Van Djick ushered them in.

"Sit gentlemen please, if you can find room in this clutter. Chunhua hasn't arrived to tidy up. Then she'll make us tea. I can put a kettle on but Chunhua's particular about her tea."

"Chunhua, funny name."

"Means Spring Flowers and the name fits."

"Never had tea before, only coffee."

"Tea is most popular in China, in fact they went to war with England twice over tea, finishing fifteen years ago."

"Why would anyone fight over something like tea, Johannes?"

"Actually Noah, they were fighting over opium. It's complicated but quickly, I think you Americans call it in a nutshell, India, a colony of England, grows the tea. Britain's empire is huge but England itself is small, not enough customers for tea. China has the people but no appetite for tea. China had a very weak emperor. In the end, England forced China to cede Hong Kong to them and forced unequal treaties giving England trading privileges. Before, China was closed to foreigners. Now stay with me, the rest of Europe now expected their fair share of trade as well and we demanded the same unequal treaties. And here we Dutch are, in Canton."

"Where does opium come into this?"

"Right. To get the Chinese interested in tea, they deviously introduced opium which is so very addictive and soon much of China is dependent on the drug."

"I think I understand. To get the opium they had to buy tea or something like that."

"Close enough, Noah."

"That is complicated, Johannes?"

Chunhua arrived with a silken swoosh, slim and lovely. She greeted them with a slight bow, an eyebrow raised in curiosity.

"Hopefully I've, how do you say, teased your curiosity. Let us enjoy our tea and some Dutch delicacies. I have a wonderful cook who has learned to make some little sweets from my homeland. Actually, from the city of Gouda famous for our cheese but these sweets compete."

"This is really good, Johannes."

"It's simple enough Jarrett, these thin layers of baked dough are the hardest for Li Na. She is now my baker as well as my cook. We call them Stroopwafels. Speaking of Li Na, have you two found a cook yet and a decent place to stay."

"That's something we need help with, any suggestions, Johannes? Captain Hartman warned us about being too close to the harbor. That's about all we know."

"It all depends on your resources, but if you're interested in my proposal which I'll explain now, you could live very well."

Chunhua refilled their porcelain cups.

"First, it could have danger but if we plan carefully with Chunhua's help, we could all make a tidy profit. Perhaps three months and by then the mandarins will have figured things out. Any questions yet?"

"Before you get into the meat of this, what's a mandarin?"

"Mandarins are public officials. There are nine levels of these officials. The problem as I see it, they are scholars well versed in Chinese classics but unprepared for daily administrative work. All are of course subservient to the emperor who nobody's allowed to see. That's another story for later. China has been around for four thousand years, the only civilization that has existed from the start.

De Jong's has decided to exclusively use Hong Kong for tulips, which will join with their other commerce. I have been offered a position that frankly gentlemen, is hard to resist. That Fragrant Harbor is only eighty miles from Canton. Now my proposition. Chunhua knows of a cache of extremely high-grade jade."

"Excuse me, Johannes, but I don't know what this jade is. How about you, Noah?"

"Me neither."

"High quality jade is an ore that competes with the price of gold and is highly coveted by artisans the world over."

"Don't know how we can help Johannes, we've only worked three jobs, cowboys for a while, sailors for a month and miners for two weeks."

"It's not the profession gentlemen, it's the trust. In your short time here in Canton, I have observed you three times, twice at Mao Mao Chung's, the first time with Captain Hartman who has earned my respect over the years, the second you know and now here in the office."

CHAPTER THIRTEEN

"Johannes, I overheard a couple of sailors at Mao's talkin' about barbarians. What's a barbarian in China?"

"Anyone who is not Chinese. They have three worlds so to speak, outsiders, big-nosed and hairy like us, themselves and finally Tien, a kind of heaven. They refer to themselves as the Middle Kingdom somewhere between barbarians and Tien. Everyone else but the Chinese are barbarians."

"Barbarian, that's what some folks call our Indians in America, I'm starting to think it might be the other way around."

They were back at the office, returning after Mao Mao Chung's and a meal of duck. Tonight, something special before starting early for the interior. Chunhua had politely declined, it would have humiliated her to be in the company of *lao wai*, foreigners.

"Meant to ask Chunhua, what's the language she speaks? I know it's Chinese, but is there a special name?"

"Cantonese. The North speaks Mandarin. China has one written language with two tonal interpretations of the written word. You have seen the calligraphy, chicken scratches to foreigners. If locals travel fifty miles, it is difficult and sometimes impossible to understand each other. And then all the different dialects add to the stew. One written language unites the people."

"She seems very educated."

"Chunhua is very fortunate. Her mother was concubine, like a minor wife to a mandarin. She insisted her daughter learn all she could. There were no school for girls."

"Chinese culture is complicated. Have you seen paintings of our nobility? Any work is out of the question, they grow long fingernails with shields to protect their daggers. It is rumored Xianfeng, the emperor, has fingernails twelve inches long. His wife and his concubines have feet half the size of his nails. Noble women bind their feet, very painful, starting when they are small children. Chinese men have a fetish for these small feet. It's very cruel."

"Don't think Chunhua has bound her feet, she doesn't shuffle when she walks."

"She doesn't. If all women bound their feet, no work would be accomplished. It is time to rest now, you are off before dawn."

Chunhua, Jarrett and Noah had successfully completed three expeditions. They had followed the Pearl River some two-hundred miles into the interior on rutted, difficult roads and then up a narrow goat track, struggling deeper into the hills. Noah was thinking bandit country. A small wagon with their supplies was pushed or pulled by a donkey named Mr. Smith. This was their last trek. Chunhua's secret stockpile of jade was finished.

"Noah and I've been wondering Chunhua, how did you know about all this high-quality ore?"

"My mother was second wife to a powerful man who found this hoard of jade surveying for the government and kept it secret for what you Americans say, a rainy day. With the Taiping revolution going on for fourteen years my father was afraid things would get worse and they did. He told my mother this secret in case something bad happened to him."

At six feet and foreign, it was impossible to hide what they were. Chunhua had a strategy. Jarrett and Noah were now American scientists on an expedition to survey and map the hinterland. They carried maps and instruments. Chunhua, dressed as a young boy was their guide. After their meals around small fires, Chunhua mentored the Americans. The subject tonight was poverty.

"China has suffered a rebellion finally finished fifteen years ago. Our scholar gentry say twenty million dead, our land ravaged and we have not the resources to improve quickly. This Taiping Revolution has devasted my country."

Headed back on the road two days from Canton, three sloppy soldiers halted them. Their intentions obvious, robbery and more. Arrogant, slovenly and careless, they demanded papers they couldn't read and started on the wagon rudely throwing what they thought valueless away, discarding worthless rock.

After smashing the instruments and ripping up the maps, they turned their attention to the boy, chastising him for guiding *lao wai*.

The leader slapped Chunhua, loosening her hair.

"What do we have here, a girl."

Number one soldier dragged Chunhua into some trees, then quickly a horrible scream. The other two chuckled, expecting the same sport. Number two soldier kept his rifle on the Americans, while number three finished his inspection.

"What's taking Zhang so long?"

With one soldier in the woods with Chunhua and one guarding the scientists the other went to investigate what was taking the first so long. Alone and confused, the remaining soldier shouted to his mates, only silence his answer.

Jarrett and Noah had been slowly separating adding more pressure on the soldier-bandit. A gunshot fired from the side of the road took away his attention and the remaining outlaw was quickly overwhelmed, smacked senseless by Noah. As they were rushing to help Chunhua, she emerged with two rifles.

"Chunhua, we heard the scream?"

"He was very soft, that one. I always have my knife, he didn't expect."

"Then you played possum and tricked the second one. Glad she's on our side, Noah. And our friend here?"

"Leave him Jarrett, if we take him to the authorities we will be buried in, what you call red tape. No, then we would have to explain why we were out here. Too many complications, maybe years. We have finished what we came for, let's tie our friend and reload the jade. He'll eventually free himself and would never report us."

"And the two unlucky ones?"

"We have our shovel."

They divided the earnings after Van Djick sold the jade to De Jong LTD.

"*Hartelijk bedankt,* Jarrett and Noah. Chunhua and I've been talking things over and think it best if we pay you in tulips."

That brought a pause from the brothers.

"Well Johannes, we'd just take them to California and plant them, then probably forget to water them, thanks anyway but silver works good with us."

This brought laughs from the four partners.

"Here is your cheque made out from the Bank of England for your share and some Chinese silver coins to help you find your way to your bank. Question please, it may seem a silly one, but do you have any identification? Can you prove who you are so you can withdraw funds or make transfers?"

Looking at each other, Jarrett and Noah shrugged.

"Our thanks again, Johannes and Chunhua, Noah and I are meeting Captain Hartman at Mao's at noon, please join us. The beer is on the captain as he has two paying customers back to California."

"I wouldn't be surprised if you didn't join the crew hoisting sails or sheets, whatever you call them."

"Chunhua, we won't embarrass you with an invitation, we understand."

"You *lao wai* so wrong, as always. I will break ethnocentric tradition as Meneer and I have an understanding and will soon be leaving for Hong Kong where we'll live among the stuffy English. I will always remember you Jarrett and you Noah as my own, my very own American cowboys."

After a special meal of shrimp dumplings, rice rolls, choy sum in oyster sauce and dou hua tufa pudding with just enough to drink, Jarrett toasted the couple with a baijiu liquor. "The very best from Noah and me, we'll see you both again at Sunset."

CHAPTER FOURTEEN

"How 'ya like this high life, Jar?"

"Reckon a body could get used to this, Noah."

"I was thinking, Jar."

"There you go again, Noah"

"What's that, Jar?"

"Thinking doesn't seem to have bothered you much, brother."

"Real nice of Captain Hartman to fix up this place for us. A bit cramped, but good enough. What do you think about sleeping in hammocks?"

"Nice, better than that hard along the Platte and that desert before we found California."

"That Bear Lake was my favorite."

"Another thing, glad Calico didn't find our arrowheads and nuggets we had sewed in our pants and glad we kept a couple pieces of jade, maybe look back one day and remember."

"What say we give Calico a little visit when we get back to Frisco."

Jarrett and Noah shared their meals with Captain Hartman.

"Remembered this morning I have some books you might want to look at."

It was Jarrett's turn to tidy the galley, no stewards on Captain Hartman's ship. "By the time I figure where everything goes Captain, we'll make port. I'd like to fix up a rabbit and a squirrel for you but would have to build a fire on the deck."

"Took a few minutes to find these books. Here ya go, Noah. This *Tale of Two Cities* is one I think you'll like. When it was first printed, it was sailed by clippers to ports in Japan and Hong Kong even to India, wherever you could find an English reader. But it was sent monthly, one clipper and one chapter at a time. I got lucky and found the whole book on Market Street. Should have time to read it before Frisco. Here's a couple extra you might poke around with."

Back to their quarters, Noah read carefully by candlelight, commenting as he went along. It was exciting and he wanted to share with Jarrett.

The next night, "Jar, these folks in France had a revolution kinda like we had but a whole lot bloodier. They had this big knife that fell on the rich folks and chopped off their heads getting even."

"You've been at your book the last three nights straight. You're gonna burn out all the tapers."

"You have to read this, Jar. In the end this guy Sydney Carton, he gives his life for a friend."

"What are the two cities on the title?"

"London, that's in England and Paris, that's in France."

"Mrs. Pawley and Caleb would be proud of you, Noah."

After some time, "Dang!"

"What, Noah?"

"One hundred twenty!"

"Hundred twenty what?"

"Had to count three times with the hammock swaying. Hundred twenty words in his first sentence. One hundred twenty! Must be a world word record."

"Betcha can't say that three times straight."

Two days before reaching San Francisco, Noah was looking over a second book. "This book is kinda different. Never seen one like this."

Jarrett realized if he waited the answer would arrive.

"It's a *Merriam-Webster Dictionary* and it's got words but no story. Explains what all the words mean. All the words go from A to Z. Guess what's the first word, Jar?"

"American?"

"Nah, this one's got two A's to start."

"How can a word have two A's to start?"

"Dunno, but it does. It's Aardvark."

"What the hell is an Aardvark?"

"Lessee, says it's an animal. Lives in Africa."

"What's the last word?

"Wow, this has a whole bunch of Z's and a V. Wouldn't know how to say it. Have a look."

Several minutes later, "Here's that manumit word. Caleb sure knew stuff. Like to remember him, Jar."

"Always will, let's keep him alive by remembering him."

Thirty days after leaving Canton, just at noon they tied up to the wharf in San Francisco.

"Captain, Hartman, how about letting Noah and I treat you to dinner tonight."

"Thanks fellas, where shall we meet? Need a half-day to take care of business."

"We don't know what's good, any ideas."

"Do indeed. Find the Tadich Grill, it's the first restaurant opened in The City, it's on Clay Street. Is seven too late?"

"We have plenty of time to find it and seven is good, that okay with you, Noah?"

"Well, don't get yourselves shanghaied."

"Let's get up to Chinatown Jarrett and get ourselves one of those Chinese baths. Need a real cleaning after a month on the *Shirley Mae*. We can find that moneychanger and get dollars for the rest of our silver coins?"

Meeting in the sitting room an hour later, "Jar where's your beard? It was just getting to look good."

"After that steamy bath, the gal running things suggested a massage, so I tried it. Lots of rubbing and pounding on the muscles, hurt but good hurt. The Chinese been doing these massages for two thousand years. Anyway, she was blind, and you know the Chinese don't like hair much. She talked me into taking the beard off. Then she shaved me without seeing, by feel. Gave me one of those hand mirrors after, didn't recognize myself. Thought about when Sergeant Crabtree told us 'bout the captains carrying those mirrors they gifted to the Indians. Hardly imagine never seeing yourself before. When I looked, a stranger looked back."

They needed a good stretch after a month on the *Shirley Mae* and decided to walk.

"Jeez Jar, what a mess. You can have these modern cities, nothing but mud holes and horse manure probably a lot of stuff I don't recognize. Just throw their trash in the street. Must really be sloppy when it rains. Hey, there's the Bank of California, bigger than most of the others around. Must have lots of money."

The friends met just before seven. After a glass of California vino blanco and their first adventure with oysters on the half-shell, Captain Hartman suggested Pacific pan-fried sand dabs with garlic scape and warm parsley with a touch of a red wine vinegar dressing. This was anchored by earthy, rich morel mushrooms, then roasted artichokes with garlic butter, all with a generous portion of ratatouille, extra eggplant and herbs.

"Excellent my two friends, now I suggest another of California's treasures, a glass of vintage port from Sonoma." It was served with an assortment of cheeses, walnuts and dates.

"Be careful with this port, it is said to loosen tongues and warm hearts, don't know which comes first."

During dinner, Captain Hartman having caught up with the news explained the war with Mexico which had just ended.

"The crux of the conflict was President Polk wanted to add land. With that Treaty of Guadalupe Hidalgo, he got a huge hunk in the Southwest which ought to make a few states someday and his big prize is California. It will take a few years to straighten out all these changes. First the Indians, then the Spanish, the Mexicans, the Bear Flag Republic and now we Americanos. Come to think that makes five flags have waved over this state if you count the Russians up at Fort Ross."

Their education was brief and on point.

"I thank you both for the most excellent food and our talk, the life of a captain can be lonely. Set you back a bit, took a look at the bill, five dollars is a lot of dinero for three, this city is getting expensive."

"We're even Captain Hartman if we can sleep on the *Shirley Mae* tonight. And I've never known your first name."

"It's Stephen and the *Shirley Mae*'s yours for as long as we're in port, another three days."

They walked back and slept in their hammocks.

"Reckon we should spend today finding some proper clothes Noah, then get to the bank and take care of business."

Downtown, they took care of the clothes. "Glad we didn't dude up too much, Jar. Look good just not fancy like some of the men strutting the street."

"Look Noah, there's a store selling books, let's have a look. Might have one of those dictionaries you fancy."

"I asked the boss lady over there if she had a book like *Tale of Two Cities*. She showed me *Oliver Twist*. When we're through at the bank I'll buy that and a real small dictionary, one easier to lug around."

At the bank, Jarrett and Noah introduced themselves and asked to make a deposit. They presented their check and a letter from Johannes. After a short wait, they were ushered into an office, the print on the window, Vice President.

The rather stuffy-looking man rose from his chair and shook hands introducing himself, "please gentlemen, sit."

Johannes had explained their situation in a letter, and it took only a short time to take care of the identifications.

An hour later all seemed to be in order. As they left, Noah thanked Mr. Lombard for the coffee.

"Jeez Jar, we're rich! Three thousand dollars! Each! Johannes was right, jade's as good as gold. Now what do we do?"

"How did you like that coffee, Noah?"

"Me, I liked it better than Chunhua's tea, what did you think?"

"Yup, me too. Let's go find one of those coffee shops we saw on Market Street and talk things over."

"Except for the hundred dollars we each took with us we can use letters-of-credit, think I understand that. You, Noah?"

"Do. What do we need, Jarrett?"

"First, reckon we need a place to live. Like to get out of town some, maybe find one of those boarding houses where meals are served. Think Crabby and Shadow are still be at the stables? If not, we need horses. How long have we been gone, Noah?"

"Thinking on that last night some. Maybe three months, a month each way on the *Shirley Mae* and a month in China."

Back at the book shop, Noah bought his books and Jarrett discovered a newspaper, *The Californian* launched in 1846, cost two cents.

"Here's a story about a man, Snowshoe Thompson, says he skied across the Sierra last winter delivering the mail. Wonder if he saw our blue lake? Advertisements, here they are, Wells Fargo, a new bank and shipping business about ready to set up in Frisco. Here we go Noah, our old stable and places to rent. Let's go find a carriage and get directions."

The driver knew the way to the stables.

Their horses had been sold to pay their board. "Sorry fellas didn't know you'd be back and had bills to pay. Did save the Henry and that old Hawkins, just couldn't part with those and a slingshot." They purchased two geldings, a spotted Appaloosa for Jarrett and a chestnut colored Morgan for Noah. The stable man suggested Mrs. Delaney's Boarding House on the outskirts of The City. "She's a real pretty widow and nice."

Mrs. Delaney was delighted when offered a month's rent for two rooms in advance. Because of the rush for commerce and land, her price was high but fair considering demand.

"Big changes Jarrett, remember how quiet your California was when we first got to Sutter's? Our prospecting and bandito days, they were some busy. Think on Señor Nieto now and then and wonder if he got his rancho back. All because of a yellow rock that can't be used for much except maybe pretty bangles. Another thing brother, you gave me your last name and I was wondering, most folks carry three names, Mexicans probably five. Do we have a middle name?"

"Never knew one. What are you getting at?"

"The Chinese all have three names, Chunhua told me she had a name that came after Chunhua. Chen means 'The Morning, so she was Chunhua Chen. Then her last name I forgot. Indians too, like Running Like the Wind or Morning Wind in the Trees."

"And you want a middle name, Noah?"

"Nope, just thinking that's all."

"I've been thinking as well. Think we should go pay our complements to Calico Jim."

They hailed a Carriage for Hire and rode along the bawdy and boisterous streets and found The Escape. The driver talked the whole way about how dangerous the Coast had become with the newest crime wave, the Sydney Ducks, Australian rift raff mostly from the port.

"Stay alert fellas, them Ducks are all over. They're serious criminals and bad news! Be careful in the saloon too."

"Don't think they'll recognize us, Noah; we look a little more refined than we did. And watch what we drink."

"Two Boca Lagers", the beers slid down the bar without losing foam. A different bartender and 'Camptown Races' pounding out on the piano with cigar smoke challenging for its share of the air. Two painted ladies immediately by their side.

"Howdy ladies. Is Calico here tonight?"

This brought a laugh. "Nope, Calico ain't here tonight, don't think we'll be seeing much of him."

"Why is that?"

"You sure ask a lot of questions. Why do you want to know?"

"We owe him something, that's all."

"Well, I could probably remember easier if you stood us a drink. Think so, Lily?"

"Yeah, my memory's a little foggy without a lady's drink."

"That's better, waddaya' want to know 'bout Jim?"

"Where can we find him? Then we can pay him."

"Let's see now, I think one more would make things clear, Lily too."

The drinks delivered, this this time the beers a bit sloppy.

"Well, what about Jim?"

"Lives on the streets now, probably at Shuijiao's. What's a couple of fancies like you want with a guy like Calico? Why don't you come over to the table over there and maybe we could have some fun tonight?"

"Maybe later, one more question and here's the price of two lady's drinks."

They found Calico Jim outside Shuijiao's, a den of opium, unconscious in his own vomit, the waste of a life.

"Reckon he's already been paid, Noah."

In the carriage back to Mrs. Delaney's they watched as armed men were bashing heads causing damage to a group of men.

"What's that all about?"

"That's our 'Committee of Vigilance'. They're cleanin' up The City, nothin' but crime and corruption. They've hanged eight of them rats and expect they'll be more. Forced some politicians to resign too, even a couple up there up on Snob Hill. Good on 'em, is wot I say."

Back at the boarding house, Jarrett went to his room and Noah went to say goodnight to Mrs. Delaney.

Walking in the morning back to the stables, Noah asked Jarrett if he'd heard of the game of rugby.

"Have not."

"Watched some guys about our age playing a game on a grassy

field the other day. Looked a lot of fun. They have this ball about the size of a pineapple we were looking at in Chinatown. Talked with a couple of them when they finished. They were dirty and sweaty, and both had bloody noses, but smiling. Said they were playing rugby. I looked it up, says 'continuous play, no rest with running and tackling'. Let's go watch next Saturday. They have a clubhouse where they drink beer after the game, both teams."

One of their fellow boarders told them the way to the clubhouse, an easy walk of a mile. After the game, Noah saw the two that he had chatted up and introduced Jarrett.

"You both look like you could play this game. Why don't you guys join our club and have a go. What say you both join us next Thursday, some of us going into The City and watch bare-knuckle boxing matches out on a wharf, it's illegal but nobody seems to care."

The next day Sunday, they were relaxing in Mrs. Delaney's lounge reading her paper.

"Look here Jarrett, says John C. Freemont is running for senator. Says he's a Republican, whatever that is. Freemont was that guy on that so-called scientific expedition stirring up the Indians, the Mexicans and the Anglos. And another thing, Mrs. Delaney said that our new president Zachary Taylor only lasted a year, died from eating cherries. Millard Fillmore took his place as our thirteenth president."

"Thirteen already, seems we just got started. Hope it doesn't bring bad luck."

"Noah, we've been in Frisco for three months now. Got that itch again. Waddaya' think?"

"Except for the rugby club and Mrs. Delaney, I'm bored Jarrett. Where we goin' now?"

"Can't get that Sonoma country out of my mind, but first, if Mrs. Delaney will let you, how about what we were thinking before we got shanghaied."

"Mean the South Road along the ocean to Monterrey?"

"We'll have to get us new possibles, it'll be good to git again."

Jarrett was ready. Noah was late, very unlike him. Mussed and sleepy-eyed, he arrived a bit sheepish. They had agreed to meet early morning at the stables. Noah had business to finish.

"Sorry I'm late Jarrett, glad we got our goods together last night."

Off again, twenty-one years and almost bearded.

"This beach is really nice Jar, plenty fresh water from this stream and plenty wood for the fire. Ocean didn't seem as salty as that salty lake. Waves a lot of fun, tossed us around like those horses in Denver. Think these waves ever been to Canton?"

"Reckon they have over the millions of years. The sleeping's good too, lot softer than coming to California."

"Millions of years, you reckon?"

"From what I understand, most Christian folk think that Bishop Ussher had it all figured out, believing that Adam and Eve left Paradise on Sunday, twenty-three October, 4004 BC. Noah and I used to talk about this, when we would be out checking the vineyards. Dad was critical of that date. It couldn't explain away those gigantic, fossil-boned dinosaurs that professor found in Montana or that German skull that's different but so similar to ours. Those creatures had to have lived a lot longer than six thousand years ago. This world we're standing on might be billions of years old."

Noah was fixing dinner after Jarrett had caught a sand bass in the surf. "Good you bought that rod and reel, going to come in handy. Got frijoles and tortillas for your pescado, Jarrett."

"Hear that talk a while back Noah, about Joaquin Murrieta? Hombre reminded me of us and the vaqueros. Supposed to be a bandito."

"Heard he was up at the diggings, a peaceful vaquero. Miners accused him and his brother of stealing a mule which Murrieta denied. Anyway, they hung his brother and horsewhipped Murrieta then raped his wife. Another story, the Anglo miners found out he had a rich claim and when he wouldn't turn it over to them, they tied him up and forced him to watch as they raped his wife."

"And now he's finding his own kinda justice, the only justice his kind can get."

"Someone oughta write a book about him one day."

The next morning, they let the sun wake them, later than usual.

Noah sitting up and rubbing sleep from his eyes asked Jarrett if he knew what time it was.

"Not exactly. Breakfast time is all I know."

"Know it's morning. Just wondered. Never had a timepiece. Never needed one."

"Then why did you ask?"

"What if I had to meet a lady, how would I know?"

Jarrett was stumped again.

"Not important out here. The sun wakes us and our stomach tell us it's eating time."

"If there was a cantina around, I'd order some frijoles, tres huevos revueltos, papas y café."

"Could we have chilaquiles as well?"

"Open up them beans, Noah."

"Talking about time, all you need a timepiece for is when you gotta catch a stage or a boat."

"Or a lady."

"Verdad."

"That telegraph is really something Jar, messages are sent over wires hung between places far away. Tap some kinda code on a machine and it comes out on another machine far away. All on a piece of paper, done in minutes."

"Folks in Monterrey will be able to talk in code someday, maybe as far away as London or Paris without yelling."

"Don't get too crazy on me, Jar."

Riding into Monterrey, they found the telegraph lady who sent their message requesting funds. She told them to return in an hour. Time for a cerveza in the plaza, then they collected their dollars from the bank.

"Did you hear that lady telling her little boy about a cute furry creature that has got himself mostly hunted out?"

"Did. Said there were hundreds out in the bay here. That's what's happening to the buffalo."

"Life sure has changed since San Luis. Don't feel much useful just wandering forever but I still got some of that itch we had when we left to come see California. Hear there's some old missions down south like Sonoma's we might want to take a look at."

"Let's see the presidio here and the wharf before we go. And then some more of that good seafood."

The next morning, they were on the path of the padres and after some leisurely days on El Camino Real rode up to the Mision de La Purisma Concepcion de la Santisma Virgen Maria. They stopped for a visit.

"Those old Spaniards sure took a lot of names to call a place."

"Looks pretty old Jarrett, and it must be Sunday, church is about to start."

"Remember up in Sonora they told us they're Franciscans, some kinda Catholics. Go to church every day, the women at least. Let's go. Never been in a Catholic Church. Hear they got a bunch of rules and a lot of ups and downs. Take off our hats and just follow what the folks do."

After the ceremony, the gente were pleased the two Anglos tried their Spanish and were generous with their friendship.

"Did you happen to see those Indians hanging around, Noah? Didn't look so good, sad-faced and very poor."

"Did, saw some in Monterrey as well, all looked the same, kinda beaten down."

They took a week exploring some beautiful bays and coastline, following trails south and east a bit and then the Mission Santa Barbara.

"Pretty down here Noah. Much like el Norte, some drier, same oak trees."

"Looks the same kinda ranchos down here too."

"They're never gonna run out of oaks. The vaqueros told us that the Indians crack open the acorns and smash the nut inside to make a kinda mush."

"Right. Can't eat the acorn the way it is, gotta soak it in water over and over to get the bad bitter out. Then cook it all on hot rocks."

"Very clever."

"What's the Indian name for that food, Noah?"

"Vaqueros said they called it *wiiwish*."

"I could do a little *wiiwish* Jar, let's go at that food the nice folks at the mission gave us."

"This bread is still warm, I'll rip off a hunk, here you go."

"They said they make this cheese from cow's milk. Didn't know there was any other til they said cheese could be made from goats, even sheep's milk. Wonder, how do you milk a sheep?"

As they were cleaning up, a farm wagon slowed and stopped.

"Howdy folks, climb on down, just finishing. We have some bread and a little cheese you're welcome to. Fair stream right behind that oak."

"Thank you, brother we have plenty. Just about to offer you the same, fresh from the mission."

"The sun is high and it's warm. We'll wait a bit before we ride on."

Two women climbed down, one a few years older. Smiling shyly, they settled themselves in the shade.

"These are my wives, Sister Rebecca and Sister Ruth. I am John."

"Nice to meet you folks. Name's Noah and my brother Jarrett, where you headed?"

"We are travelling east, perhaps another week or two to our home in the south of Deseret."

"Don't know Deseret."

"It is a new nation founded by our church president, Brigham Young, our Moses. In 1847 he led one hundred fifty of us to what you call Utah travelling the Glory Road from Nauvoo in Illinois. We settled at Salt Lake."

"Spent a piece looking around that big salty some, been that Glory Road as well."

"A very big coincidence, if you had stayed you might have become one of us, a Latter-day Saint."

"Might have, but when we were there you weren't. Noah and I must have been there a bit earlier, summer of forty-seven.

"Sisters Rebecca, Ruth and I left Salt Lake to spread our faith as far as California. Our home is only a four-day wagon ride from Los Angeles."

"This is getting mighty interesting. Then how did you get to California?"

"We joined a small train of wagons from Salt Lake northwest to Fort Hall, then on to Oregon City. Providence shined on us and we hooked on with another group south to California. And here we are a year later. Only a few days more to our new home. Some settlers from Salt Lake are there now. They took the easy route south."

"And here we are right out of the Bible, John, Noah, Rebecca, and Ruth, sorry Jarrett.".

"They all shared a laugh at the irony."

CHAPTER FIFTEEN

The census of 1850 listed 1,650 residents. Jarrett and Caleb were apprehensive visitors as they toured the pueblo.

"Been here a week now, pretty wild town Jarrett. Here's another big church, don't seem to run out of those. Look at the official name on the wall here, El Pueblo de Nuesta Señora la Riena de Los Angeles. Now that's a big name for a little town. If anybody asked where ya from, take half a day to tell 'em. Lots of churches all over town, wish people would act the way the church teaches."

The U.S. Army was in control of Los Angeles supervising the change from Mexican to American. After the arrival of federal troops, the pueblo was submerged in lawlessness. A thuggish New York regiment responsible for maintaining order were themselves little more than brawlers, joined by the scoundrels of the town. Los Angeles had the reputation of being the most lawless city west of Santa Fe and the toughest town in America.

"Quiet in town tonight."

"I'm confused, when we were talking about the Gold Rush with those gents yesterday, one of those fellas said that Los Angeles supplied beef for hungry miners at the diggings calling Los Angeles, The Queen of the Cow Counties. How come they don't eat their own beeves already up there?"

"Don't know about beeves, but do know the army's policing Los Angeles, seen no other law around. Mexicans all seem beaten down. Real bullies last night harassing those brown folks looking for rooms."

"There's talk going around about a bandito, Juan Flores. Aims to pay back all the gringos and make this Mexico again. That bald guy at the cantina last night asked, 'if he liked Mexico so much, maybe be oughta go back there'. What he doesn't realize, Juan Flores was probably born here, maybe his folks too. Been here longer than that guy anyway."

Juan Flores, Joaquin Murrieta and Saloman Pico, a cousin to Pio Pico, the last Mexican governor of Alta Californio, believed this land was for their people. No Anglos allowed! A folk hero among the Mexican gente, to the whites a thief and an outlaw akin to what Jessie James would become in twenty-five years. These insurrectos helped create a long-lasting suspicion toward the Mexican. Their gang, Los Manillas or Handcuffs, had Anglo Los Angeles nervous. Three weeks later, Juan Flores was hanged in front of 3,000 spectators. Spanish language street names were being changed to English, a rush to anglicize Los Angeles.

"Caleb might have something to add to this crazy, Jar. Everyone's forgotten the Indian. California's first folk at the bottom of this human pile."

"Sad Noah, but can't spend today complaining about yesterday, won't make things better tomorrow".

"You're the philosopher now, Jar. Let's have dinner at Nelly's, down by the river tonight. You can philosophize me some more."

Nelly's was popular, waiting an hour for a table.

"This chile relleno is perfecto, how's your carne asada?"

"Best ever."

"Señora, por favor, what is the name for your river?"

"Oh, Señor, it has twelve names, we just call it El Rio. Over here I have a paper with names, you can look yourself."

"El Rio de Nuestra Señora La Riena de los Angeles de Porciuncula. Says it's fed by all the tributaries coming down from the mountains."

After the meal they took the short walk to the plaza on Olvera Street. Listening and watching mariachis with señoritas promenading, they drank a few tequilas too many.

"What do you do first, I can never remember the salt or the lime?"

"Forget as well, Jar. Probably do it different every time."

"What I do know is Los Angeles is going to stay a pueblo Jar, won't grow like Frisco."

"¿Porque'?"

"Not enough water. That little river's never gonna take care of many more folks. Gotta drink, cook, wash and then use the water to take the filth away. Might flood in the wet but there's no lake to catch it. Right down to the ocean."

"And all that water in El Norte and few folks to use it. Don't like it much here, Jarrett, let's move on."

"Heard if we continue south along the ocean we'll bump right into another mission. Back where we went to church, they talked about a mission south of Los Angeles in the pueblo San Juan Capistrano. Supposed to be special, let's ride down that way and find out. And it's is on the way to San Diego. The padres supposed to walk between these missions in a day."

"Must be fast walkers."

"Don't have to carry much, supposed to stay unrich, don't know the word. Look it up for me tonight, will ya, Noah?"

"Doesn't work that way, Jar, have to know the word before you can look it up. I'd have to read the whole book to find it."

"No hurry, Noah."

"If Los Angeles had a Chinatown, we could get one of those baths and a massage."

After three easy half days of riding along the ocean, sharing the other half in the surf, they entered the courtyard of the mission San Juan Capistrano.

An Indian woman was struggling with a load of wood, carrying it as best she could. Jarrett dismounted, handing the reins to Noah and relieved the woman of her burden following her to the mission cookhouse, a gracias and a de nada exchanged.

That next dawn Jarrett woke nauseas with stomach pain and sweating excessively.

"Problem, Jar?"

"Something got me. Carrying that wood yesterday, think maybe I got bit by a snake or a spider or a wasp or something. The inside of my arm is all red and swollen. I'm really weak and sick to my stomach."

"We're just outside the mission, let's go find if they have a doctor."

Walking unsteady into the mission they followed the smells from the cookhouse. The same Indian and two Mexican women were there tending the early morning fire and gossiping.

Jarrett showed them his arm.

"Go quickly and get Maria and tell her to bring her medicines. I think it's the bite of the Widow."

Maria was a curandera, a healer. Using traditional remedial herbs along with some quiet Catholic ritual, Jarrett was doctored, his arm wrapped in linen. Another gracias and another de nada.

Two mornings later, a fit Diego found the healer with the women tending the cookhouse fire and presented them with two fresh pescados.

"Real pretty here, Jar. When we first arrived, the lady selling flowers told us that nice story about all those swallow birds leaving and then a whole year later they all come flying home, thousands."

"Those two birds, Valentina and Isabella, we met are the ones who interest me mostly. Hard to figure women and double hard to figure señoritas. They're flirty, really know how to use their eyes and then they cool off, just when you try to get extra friendly, know what I mean? Even if they do get amiable, those aunties always show up at the wrong time."

"Know their folks would never approve of a gringo in the family."

"Wasn't thinking of marrying, Jar."

"WHA---there we go again, that one wasn't so bad, scary when the ground starts moving around like that. Those old missions could be in trouble one of these days."

Riding south after a day, "Jar, think ever be folks settling around here?"

"What would anyone do except maybe cowboy?"

"Farm, but only for themselves. No folks around to buy anything. Los Angeles and San Diego too far away. This will just stay empty of folks, and that's the way it oughta stay. The missions have their own farms, that's where all the Indians seem to live. Mexicans don't seem interested in commerce, at least California Mexicans. The Spanish and Mexicans never needed banks, just traded for things. That's the way I see it."

"Then Marshall finds gold."

Baja California, when first visited in the sixteenth century by Spanish conquistadors was thought to be a large island instead of a peninsula. As the explorers continued north, they eventually divided California between the lower, baja and northern, alto. California was the name of a fictional island ruled by Queen Califia and her black warrior women, described by Garci Rodriguez de Montalvo in his novel *Las Sergas de Esplandian*. It seemed the perfect name.

They had beautiful and robust bodies, and were brave and very strong. Their island was the strongest in the World, with its steep cliffs and rocky shores. Their weapons were golden and so were the harnesses of the wild beasts that they were accustomed to taming so they could be ridden, because there was no other metal in the island than gold.

CHAPTER SIXTEEN

San Diego was smaller than The City of the Angels with five hundred or so living in a slumberous pueblo.

"Nice around here Jar, nobody in any hurry. No sense hurrying if there's nothing to hurry to. Besides it's warm."

"There you go again, Noah."

"Someday, they'll build here on the water, trying to be a Frisco with restaurants selling those crabbys and shrimps." Then they found a small cantina just opening its door.

"Buenos tardes Señores, por favor sientate. My name is Sebastion, do you speak some Spanish?"

"Poco Señor. This is Jarrett and I am Noah."

Jarrett and Noah were his only patrons. Taking the opportunity to ask questions, Noah started.

"Just rode down from el Norte, and don't know much about San Diego. Do know you have a mission."

"Si, the mother of all of them. Padre Junipero Serra started here in San Diego, now twenty-one of them all the way to Sonoma."

"Did Father Serra discover California?"

"No, that was Juan Cabrillo, a captain of ships. He landed here in 1542. It wasn't until 1602 that our pueblo was called San Diego, some sixty years later. We use that word discover loosely I'm afraid, El Indios already had found California many years before we Spaniards. We have a little cancioneta about the captain, I think you say, a ditty,

'Cabrillo sailed the ocean blue
In fifteen hundred forty-two.'

Silly, a little rhyme for the children. The captain is rumored to have died and is buried on an isla off Los Angeles he named San Salvador. Today it is called Catalina."

"Don't mean to be rude Sebastian but how do you know your history so good?"

"Ah, I have this little restaurante that I open after siesta. In the mornings I work at the mission, I am what you call a bibliotecario. If you have time mañana, ride over to the mission. I will be there late morning, no reason to hurry in this life. I will show you some books and we can talk about the first days of Spanish California."

An hour before noon, they arrived at the mission.

"Hola amigos, come in, come in por favor. Café and some pan dulces and then maybe a little story for you. Maybe our Padre Serra."

"It will turn hot soon, so just a sketch to his memory. And then a taste of some vino. We grow the grapes and make it here at the mission. Our Indios do the work for us. A secreto between us. Officially, we Spanish have evangelized their souls but sometimes I wonder if the price has been too expensive for them. Along the way, we have taken their spirit as well as their souls. But I am a persona secular, not a churchman. Our critics even accuse us of slavery. Good for me the Inquisition is history.

Another café then a short history lesson. Nueva España es perfecto por colonization. California so mismo, a duplicar. Our grapes, oranges, lemons, figs grow and cattle graze, muy similar. Nueva España once all the way to those mountains you call the Rockies. And for the padres, all those souls to save. Now that is all America."

"And Padre Serra?"

"It is warming. So quickly, Junipero Serra was a Franciscan friar who personally founded the first nine missions. He is buried just norte of Monterrey. I think it important to know that a mission is more than a church, a mission controls much land and many Indios."

"One last question and then a taste of your vino. What is a Franciscan?"

"A religious order founded by St. Francis of Asissi and known for their preaching. Follow now to our cellar and some vino tinto, it is cool there. A Spanish toast amigos, 'Salud y dinero y todo tiempo para disfrutario.'

¿A donde vas ahora, señores?"

"We got this itch, a picar Sebastian. Mexico maybe."

"I am rarely hurried myself, if you feel the same, I'll open my place early mañana, say diez. We can drink a little café and I will bring some pan dulces, I have another little tale for you, mucho interesante."

"You came, a complement for me, gracias."

"And gracias to you, Sebastian."

"Drink up amigos, while the café is hot, and the day is still cool. I wanted to share one last story. In Tejas, at the Battle of the Alamo, the General Antonio Lopez de Santa Anna lost a leg and transported it in his own wagon to The City of Mexico. El Presidente Santa Anna had his leg buried in a State Funeral. When he does die for sure, a second memorial. Two funerals for one man. Our talks have been about Californio, but I wanted to share this amusing story. Now, go have a siesta before your next adventura. Come back and visit our little pueblo, vaya con dios, amigos."

"The bay's sure pretty but not much around. Someone will figure a way to use this. Too perfect not to have boats. Don't know where they'd come from, maybe Mexico. Be something to see the *Shirley Mae* with Captain Hartman docked here."

"Well Noah, we've run out of California, want go home to San Luis?"

"Don't think so, been thinking."

"Of course, what this time?"

"Let's elect for Mexico."

"I elect for Mexico as well, after all she's the mother of California."

"Then let's howdy Mother."

They didn't know what to do at the official crossing, so they rode their horses east a few miles and crossed the frontier into Mexico.

"Noah, we've got our possibles and plenty agua and our Spanish is decent. Just carry on like we know what we're doing."

"Funny thing?"

"What's that, Noah?"

"The border."

"What about the border?"

"Just a line, can't see it but it's there, separating folks."

"Correct."

"Nothing changes, still the same land on both sides, just different countries."

They rode into San Miguel at sunset and tied their horses in front of the cantina that had seen no good days.

The gente, suspicious of the Anglos were distant but polite.

"These folks are poor, Jar. Drink up, let's camp outside this pueblo."

Twenty worn soldados rode into town. leaving his men in the street, an officer entered the quiet cantina.

"Buenos tardes, amigos. I see you are visiting my country. bienvenidas."

"Hola, Capitán. ¿Como esta'?"

"I am Captain Bojorquez, let me buy you a tequila. They charge me, but I don't pay. It is a little game we play. That way I protect them."

"Protect 'em from who, Capítan?"

"From themselves."

An hour before dawn they were on their way back to California.

"Didn't trust that captain last night, glad we left, had one of those feelings."

"As well, Jar."

Crossing the border where they had entered, they paused looking back. "Adios, Madre."

"Let's go home, Jarrett."

"San Luis?"

"Nah, California, home's up there someplace."

CHAPTER SEVENTEEN

"What's that book like that Sebastian gave you to read?"

"*Two Years Before the Mast* is a story about a common sailor on a two-year sea voyage from Boston to California. A lot tougher than our little adventure across the Pacific. These sailors had to sail round Cape Horn, terrifying storms, icebergs and foul weather for weeks and weeks climbing up and down the masts, all that with a toothache. More than a month sometimes to sail an inch on a map.

They finally get to Mexican California and trade for hides in San Diego, San Pedro, Santa Barbara, Monterrey and Frisco, when all that was Mexico. But the book is important because it tells the way those sailors were mistreated. Written by a guy named Dana. Sebastian said he was trying to expose and change things for those sailors."

Four weeks riding easy, they took a route north through the Central Valley, then a bit east into the Sierra foothills where they happened on Groveland.

"Another boom town Noah, counted seven hotels, business must be good."

"Let's try that Iron Door saloon, looks as good as any."

"What's your poison fellas, you're the first aboard today. Just got beer delivered yesterday, name's Edgecomb, call me Ed."

"Pour us each one of those beers, Ed. Town here looks prosperous, gold I reckon."

"Correct. Groveland's been around since the start in forty-eight, was part of what they called Savage Diggins. Do have some problems now and then with some banditos raisin' hell, robbing folks, stealing horses. But mostly good."

"Reckon you'll stick around, Ed?"

"Good timing on that question. Worked in the newspaper business in Cincinnati before I caught the gold bug. Something I had to try.

Dragged my wife Susan out here. Finally figured out I had already struck gold when I found my Sue. She's the cook here. Oughta try one of the steaks and her pies are the best. Anyway, didn't do any good in the diggings, all the choice spots taken and claimed by the time I arrived. Another beer?"

"Thanks Ed."

"I have informed Mr. O'Laughlin, he's the owner of the Iron Door, that I have a position in Sacramento with the *California Star*. That Sam Brannan who made it so big selling wares to the miners owns the paper and he offered me a position after I mailed him my credentials."

Jarrett and Noah ate a steak and finished with a coffee and a slice of Susan's sugar cream pie.

As Susan was refilling their cups, Noah asked her about the iron doors.

"They're iron all right, installed last year after Mr. O'Laughlin brought them from England."

Just as Susan turned away from the table, one of miners brushed her arm accidentally splashing coffee from her pot.

"Sorry I spilled your coffee, ma'am."

"Oh, you didn't spill it. The pot spilled it."

'That's awful generous of you ma'am. Never thought of it that way."

"Always thought that life is like that pot. If you get a bump in life, what will spill out, humility or pride?"

After camping outside of town, they headed east climbing a winding path.

"Thinking back to when we left San Luis looking for moss on trees and that bright star of yours."

"We were green as that moss, Jar."

"This seems a decent trail Noah, let's see what happens."

Riding easily through a gentle forest with the oaks left behind, the trees changing to a mix of cedar and pines with an occasional larger reddish tree with fibrous bark, they approached a large meadow and were mildly surprised with sheep grazing and a shepherd sitting on a flat rock, whittling on a branch.

"Howdy, names Jarrett, my brother, Noah."

"And a good day to you gentlemen. Welcome, names John. What brings you here, if I may ask?"

"My brother and I are heading home wherever that is. Beautiful here."

"That it is, hope you're not thinking of settling here."

"Wasn't considering here, maybe up in Sonoma some place. What's wrong with here, John?"

"Nothing, that's the problem Noah, it's too nice and people will spoil it, that's all."

"Then we'll have a quick look around here and head up north a way."

"No offense, just really partial to these mountains. I was about to brew a cuppa', care to join me. I buy my tea in any of those Chinese camps that have sprouted during the gold craziness. My kettle is right over here, sit, please."

"Haven't had tea in a while, John. May I ask where you're from? Not a whole lot of Californian's drink tea and you sound a bit different from folks around here."

"Scotland to start with Jarrett, then my folks farmed in Wisconsin, the year it became part of the union, 1848. Now California."

"Then you've only been in California a couple years, same with us. Noah and I came here from Colorado. Seems the only folks natural here are the Indians."

"Here comes Abarran, he's been here longer than all of us. Abbran's a Basque from Northern Spain and a natural sheep man. If you have some days to spare, I'll show you a special place, but you must promise me you won't make it your home. Abarran will watch and take good care of our goods."

Two days they rode through more forest.

"Now we wait a few minutes and grab our breaths, because we will need it."

"Damn!"

Not to swear Noah, you are now in church."

"Sorry John, it's just I've never seen, never expected to see anything like this, look at all those waterfalls, Jar."

"And that mountain with half it gone!"

"And that rock wall. Is there a name for a place like this, John?"

"The Indians call it Yosemite. Sad name for a wondrous place. Means 'those who kill', named for the Indians who lived here. They were feared by the surrounding Miwok tribes. Don't spread the word about Yosemite, I'm afraid that someday folks by the score will invade and then it's ruined. Now we'll camp and then another special experience.

"We'll take a few days and ride about thirty-five miles up and out of the valley for your next experience, hope you're not in a hurry."

"Don't say it Noah, I will. Dang! Worth that three-day ride and a lot more John, what to call these beauties?"

"Sequoias Jarrett, maybe the largest trees in the world and older than the time of Jesus. See those black scars? They are on every mature tree. Lightning has struck every single one at least once. If I had the time, we could have another epiphany at Hetch Hetchy, but past time to get back to Abarran and the sheep."

"What's this Hetch Hetchy, John?"

"It's another Yosemite Noah, every bit as stunning. Hetch Hetchy means 'Kind of Wild Grass' to the Miwok."

"Did God make all this, John?"

"He did in his way, Jarrett. See those big snow fields up higher in the mountains. Those are glaciers, huge, heavy sheets of ice. They move slowly and relentlessly. That's what carved this valley, all this grandeur with His approval. I have a serious critic, however, Mr. Josiah Whitney, a young professor from Harvard University. Mr. Whitney's convinced other forces made these places. He calls me a mere sheepherder and ignoramus. Has letters after his name so they'll probably name a mountain for him someday."

"How long ago did all this happen, John?"

"This sheet of ice, I calculate maybe thirty thousand years ago. Same time the Indian arrived in North America."

"Wish we had time to hear that story."

Back with the Basque, they shared a meal of mutton, vegetables with a jug of red wine that Abarran had found somewhere.

"We've seen a bit of California John and looking to see more. Noticed almost everywhere the land rolls with hills and then mountains, mountains everywhere we go."

"Mr. Whitney would call that basin and range country and you're correct, no matter where you ride, you'll find mountains. That's why Yosemite is so special."

"We'll be off at first light, John. Thanks for the special treat.

Jarrett and I feel very privileged to share your wonder. Abarran, thank you for the meal and watching our goods."

As they rode away from camp Jarrett asked, "Noah did we ever learn John's last name?"

"Forgot to ask."

"As well. Seems more than a shepherd."

"Do you have that little dictionary in your saddlebag?"

"Do."

"Would you look up that word epiphany?"

"Already have."

"Well, what's the word mean?"

"Forgot."

"Come on, Noah."

"Means a religious experience."

"Got that right."

A new trail back west and then north took them through the settlements of Coarsegold, Angels Camp, Hang Town, mostly tented villages.

"Street's sure muddy this morning, how 'bout some flapjacks, Jar? There's a tent with that big sign. Ouch, four dollars each, now that's steep."

"Would you call that perpendicular prices?"

"And, ya gotta wait in line."

"That store last night was selling eggs for three dollars each and shovels for thirty-six. Señor Nieto was right, that's the way to get rich."

"Wonder how much a whore cost? They're in all the cantinas, but never asked."

"Reckon wherever you find a bunch of men chasing after gold you're gonna find a lot of ladies chasing after men."

"At least the men with the gold."

Gambling was evident as they rode along the street out of town. New boomtowns starting wherever a new strike was discovered, Jamestown, Murphys, Auburn.

Word of a mountain of gold reached Hong Kong. In three years, twenty-five thousand Celestials, as these immigrants were called, found their way to California, many to the diggings and the railroad. San Francisco was the port of entry. Americans did not welcome these competitors and with the Anti-Coolie Act of 1862, California placed a steep monthly tax on the workers giving them no choice but to pay if they wished to work. Five million dollars were added to the state's coffers. Not a Chinaman's Chance in Hell signified the negative sentiment on the West Coast.

The railroad used these underpaid laborers for particularly dangerous jobs like lowering them in flimsy baskets to place precarious nitroglycerin to blast holes for the tracks. Low wages left them scant money to send home.

All this somehow led to the belief that this Yellow Peril was a danger, thinking no jobs would be left for Americans.

In San Francisco, a renowned Cantonese prostitute, Miss Ah Toy had the nerve to take an Anglo to court after he threatened her, something she never could have done in China. Her new country had given her a hint of republicanism, even without citizenship.

Working at reduced wages, many Chinese women were forced into prostitution.

Not allowed to start political organizations the Chinese remained without power.

Tongs, associations created to handle the affairs of residents in a booming Chinatown took care of legal matters, criminal enforcement, banking and aid for the immigrants. Competitive and often dangerous, Tongs controlled much of San Francisco Chinatown reaching far into the hinterland. Tong simply means 'hall' or 'a gathering place', the organization a lot more.

To fund their endeavors, they turned to practices like gambling, prostitution and opium which were legal in China.

"John was right, Jar."

"What's that?"

"This here Hangtown. A couple things, the hills are disappearing, washed away. The mountains are being ruined. Look over there, the whole half of that big hill is all washed away hunting for gold. Placer mining with those high-powered hoses. They oughta change the name, call this place Placerville.

And over there, the whole place. No conscience! Can't grow them hills back. A lot different from when men went to the streams, with pans, big business now."

"And the other?"

"The Chinese, the way their treated. Can't help but feel sorry for them, see the miners bullying them. Makes me wonder why they came here in the first place."

"Dreams Noah, dreams. The same ones we had for California."

They continued north and another tented boomtown.

"How about getting these rags in our saddlebags clean, been a little ranky since San Diego. We can clean the ones we're wearing in Sacramento."

"There's a laundry tent just there."

"Howdy, would you clean these for us?"

"Yes, come in, please. Not much work yet. I have ready, one hour. You wait, come back, okay."

"We'll wait if it's okay. I have a question please, wondering if you've ever been to Canton?"

"I came from Hong Kong, very close to Canton. My name is Wei, but everyone calls me Wong, they call all of us Wong, other names too hard on tongue. They have little joke, 'two Wongs don't make a white.'"

With their clothes dried and pressed, a *do xia* with a slight bow from Jarrett as he paid the bill. "We lived in Canton for a short time and always wondered about your pigtails. Would you mind me asking?"

"No, but first, there is no more work, so please, sit on those barrels, I soon have tea for us."

"In the first decades of the Qing Dynasty, you say Manchu, they force Han, pure Chinese people, to wear queue or pigtail to tell difference. We look same. Han, now less prestige than Manchu. After time, all started wearing queue. Whoever conquers China eventually become Chinese, like the Manchus and Mongols."

"What was your work in Hong Kong, Wei, you speak English so easily."

"I worked for a Dutch trading company as clerk."

"Would that be De Jongs?"

"Yes, but how, how would you know De Jongs?"

"It's a long story Wei and here come some customers."

"And I have some small business in Angel's Camp tomorrow, and my mule is slow. I will ask you when we meet in Tien."

They rode away towards Sacramento.

"Forgot to ask how Hangtown got its name. Must be their law and order at the end of a rope."

They entered Sacramento after three easy rides.

"Grown some and we've only been away a while."

"Let's find a hotel and they can take care of our dirty clothes. We can go to a bank in the morning."

"Keep forgetting, we're men of substance. There's one, the Double Eagle. Looks like they just finished building it. Let's find a stable then check in."

"Asked the lobby man about bookstores when we came down. Said I was lucky. A man, name's Anton Roman, got rich in the diggings and one thing he did was open Sacramento's first bookstore. With seven thousand folks, he's bound to sell a lot of papers. Two cents for every one, gonna add up."

"Wonder if it'll slow when the gold slows."

At the bookstore, Jarrett asked, "Find anything you like yet, Noah?"

"Have. *David Copperfield,* just new this year. That pretty lady behind the counter, the one, wearing the glasses said it was about an hombre in London. Said it might be hard to read just like *Tale of Two Cities.* First came out in what she called serials, a month at a time, with the newspapers. Learned that on the *Shirley Mae.*"

"A newspaper here, *The Bee.* Funny name. Something about India here, *Indian Soldiers Mutiny Against the English.* Like our revolution, seems everyone's mad at the English these days."

"Funny, Indians in India."

The two amigos exploring their options as they rode north, loafed in Sonoma a few days.

"Still like this Sonoma, Noah. We've seen some, all the way to Mexico, not everyplace but enough for me for now. Asked around and prices are high, lots of prospectors staying in California, still gold crazy.

Those businessmen who never went to the streams probably did better than most of the miners. Even the gamblers got a share of the riches. Fella I was talking with about land around here said that Samuel Brannan, that's the guy that Ed at the Iron Door said owned the newspaper, made the most. Sold stuff to the miners, sometimes five thousand dollars in one day. Said the Mormons ended up kicking him out of their church after a lot of shenanigans."

"Same fella also said he was the one that let the cat out of the bag, shouting out GOLD! GOLD! And that was after a fifty-mile ride from Sutter's Mill and then the ferry to Frisco."

"No secret about the land around here. Costs three to five dollars an acre some places. Might go even higher. Reckon it's the time to buy. Thanks to that jade we can do it, Jar. We could get our own place, but I'd like to keep this brotherhood going. Rather than two places, maybe we should buy one big one like a small ranchito. We can always live apart on the same place, might even marry one of these years."

"I'm kinda used to you, brother, let's start asking around."

And they did.

CHAPTER EIGHTEEN

Sitting on Jarrett's veranda overlooking the hills turning that summer yellow brown with oak trees generously scattered, the men reminisced after their Sunday family supper.

"Been thinking, Jar."

"Should have that down by now, Noah."

"Like you keep telling me, gotta keep practicing. Thinking about the Pony Express that brought us news and letters all the way from Missouri. That's about two thousand miles and about those boys riding it all the way to Sacramento, sometimes maybe a hundred miles in a day. Now we got the telegraph and the railroad."

"There's always something that comes along and makes things faster, not always better but mostly. This new California is changing, amigo. Our old friend Fremont ran for president awhile back for that new Republican Party that stands against slavery. It's going to get interesting. Our young ones gonna have to figure things out."

"They mostly do Noah, mostly."

"What's on that thinking brain of yours, Jarrett?"

"How we bought our ranchito and built our places a few miles apart, an easy ride to visit. And Miguel, how we found him just here from the old country, knew his vines and wines. Place doesn't do more than pay for itself, but we don't need much. Our ladies seem happy, our muchachos, five of them now."

"Seems all the little ones want to play is Cowboys and Mexicans, little vaqueros."

"Three for you and two me just like it's always been."

"Remembering how we met Yolanda and Francisca on the promenade. Folks sure not happy 'bout that, first gringos in the family. Had to promise to be Catholics and do all those ups and downs and raise the muchachos the same, took them some time to give in. Remember you telling me about Rice Christians in China who only went to church when times were bad. You called us Tortilla Christians."

"We're rich Noah, just like Señor Nieto was before they chased him away, rich with family and friends."

"Sneaky way we find excuses to miss Mass then quietly slip away fishing."

"Old folks are good, but they still wish we were browner."

"Verdad. Abuelo Mateo calls your youngest Caleb, 'Huerro'."

"All our time in California Noah, all the places we've seen, all the folks we've met, makes me feel brown at least on the inside."

"Remember you asking why some talk Spanish a little different."

"Yup, another of my slip-ups. Hadn't learned that Castilian is a more proper kind of Spanish. The folks have always referred to themselves as Castilian rather than Spanish, mismo to me but I don't say anything. Look out on the lawn, there our ladies go now, holding hands, walking and talking."

"And still more than purdysome. You call Yolanda Janey, like Captain Lewis."

"Found Sacagawea a little too clumsy."

Back and forth, Jarrett and Noah shared memories.

"Ever think of that first port we ever tried."

"That was that Frisco restaurant, can't recall the name."

"Tadich Grill."

"With captain Hartman."

"Did you read where Frisco has a king now, ours as well."

"Is Sutter back?"

"Ha, no, another one. Norton 1 has taken over Frisco, and proclaimed himself Emperor of the United States, all thirty-seven states. Not only that, he's the Protector of Mexico as well. A giggle for the folks. The emperor even prints his own money which some of the establishments honor. Reckon he's a bit loco but not loco malo. Now he's proposing crazy talk about digging tunnels under The City and even a bridge connecting with Oakland."

"Speaking of bridges, there's lots of water flowed under ours, Jar. You still have those arrowheads we found at that Bear Lake and the jade from China?

"Do, and a nugget from the American where all that crazy began and my old slingshot, and of course the Hawkins. It's hanging over there."

"Feel terrible 'bout America. Talking war in *The Herald*. We're away from most of that madness but it's still our country. California gold will probably pay for a war if there is one."

"We never got around picking middle names. Maybe I should choose yours and you mine."

"We've seen plenty Noah, done plenty, cowboys in Denver, part of the Oregon and the California Trail, escaped from Indians, banditos with the vaqueros, buried a friend, even shanghaied to China. Just remembered Caleb's story about Tecumseh's curse. With Lincoln just elected president, makes me wonder."

"Mostly good memories Jarrett, the folks here, the Arnolds and Pawleys, our sergeant, the cowboys in Denver."

"And Johannes and Chunhua who made this all possible."

"Señor Nieto and the vaqueros, even that Captain Bojoquez in Mexico."

"That good Sebastian who taught us to appreciate la cultura."

"Will always remember John who showed us and taught us about Yosemite."

"It's the folks, Noah. It's the folks who make history live."

"Don't get all weepy on me, Jar. Reckon there's some time left before Sunset."

"Would you do it again, Noah?"

"In a heartbeat."

"Salud mi hermano, thank you for coming to California. We have it all here Noah, right here," Jarrett touching his corazon.

And the boys who became men sipped their port.

BOOK TWO

SONS OF MEN

CHAPTER ONE

The American Civil War was fought from 1861 to 1865 after decades of tension between the northern states and the southern states over slavery, westward expansion and state rights. The election of Abraham Lincoln and his party's anti-slavery campaign caused eleven states to secede from the Union beginning with South Carolina to form the Confederate States of America. Nearly 750,000 soldiers lost their lives in the conflict. 360,000 soldiers from the North died in the first step to freeing Blacks from southern slavery. Black men represented ten percent of the Union Army and 40,000 perished for their own cause.

Fredrick Douglass: *"Once let the black man get upon his person the brass letter, U. S., let him get an eagle on his button, and a musket on his shoulder and bullets in his pocket, there is no power on earth that can deny that he has earned the right to citizenship."*

California played a valuable financial role funding the conflict with Sierra Nevada gold, while volunteer Californians suppressed Confederate forces securing the New Mexico territory for the Union.

The Texas Ranger was knocked off his feet, the arrow buried deeply in his heart, taking a full minute writhing and moaning to perish. Another victim of a Comanche attack by none other than Chief Buffalo Hump, the scourge of Texas and a whole lot more. Diego Andersen the most famous of all the Texas Rangers was history, the third time today. The 1840 Great Raid of Texas was postponed for another day.

"Tomorrow I get to be Buffalo Hump, Caleb."

It was almost dark, and the boys were expected home.

"When did your dad say you could have a pony, Diego?"

"Next year. It's been next year for two years now."

"Same here, dad's okay with it, it's mom, she's always saying next year."

"We're gonna be seven pretty soon, wasting our whole lives on the ground."

"Mañana Diego, already in trouble again, supposed to be home before dark."

"Talked with your folks yet, Caleb? It's our turn to go see the elephant."

"Waiting for just the right time, Diego. Think dad would be okay with leaving, it's mom that, you know, I don't want to hurt her."

"Only going to be gone a couple years."

"Problem Caleb, our moms got this hair about college. Neither of our dads even went to school, left San Luis when they were seventeen."

"Always teasing dad that they hadn't even invented schools when he was a kid."

"Let our sisters be the scholars of the family, there the smartest anyway."

"Don't even have any real schools around Sonoma anyways, or Napa either. The sisters taught us some, still have scars on our knuckles to prove it. San Francisco's has the closest real high school, been there since '60, let them go to college."

"Let's tell our dads next Sunday when we're all together for dinner."

"Good idea Diego, we'll join them on the veranda after dinner and state our plan and let them tell our moms."

"After they've had a couple ports."

And they did.

"And you want us to tell the moms? Make us the hombres malo? Was hard to tell Ellie Mae and now I gotta do it again!"

"We'll do it together Jar, the four of us."

Their idea was to see what the dads had seen of California and exploring some parts they missed. The boys expected they could find jobs on the way. Work was not new to them, their ranchito had supplied plenty of that growing up, helping old Miguel with the grapes: cane cutting, pruning, fertilizing, canopy management, erosion control, thinning, harvesting, hoeing, leafing, perimeter management, planting, root removal, shoot tipping, staking, suckering, training and tying. The boys grew up fixing equipment and taking care of their animals. By their tenth birthdays they were more than adequate horsemen.

Diego and Caleb slept past sunrise, then a breakfast of huevos, tocino, frijoles and tortillas. After a final inventory of their possibles, they rode away with an adios and a vaya con dios. Miguel saw them off with una oricion silenciosa. The boys turned their horses at the gate and waved their sombreros, then rode south.

June 1870

Diego and Caleb were seventeen with fifty dollars each, cash they had saved through their years, their saddlebags stuffed with jerky and beans.

"Let's ride over to Napa and see if those Prieto girls are still around. Maybe they're looking for a little divertida."

The next day, the cousins were on the southern road towards Sacramento, "Wondering Diego, if we stayed, we could have some of fun with those Preito sisters."

"Si, they're nice but did you notice, at least Margarita, serious and kind of old fashioned, expects me to court the old way. Hard time telling her I wasn't interested in courting. And I don't want to pretend. Sometimes I think I'm not, but I am, I'm still a kid, not ready to marry. Have to see the elephant first."

"Before we left home, mom talked about how I wasn't prepared for life without school. I told her I had seventeen years of experience working the rancho and she told me that I had one year's experience seventeen times."

"Let's call our dads by their names from now on, Diego."

"Buena idea, cousin."

Their thinking was to skirt Sacramento a little to the east, find a ford on the Sacramento River then ride southeast to the Sierra foothills and follow the Gold Road south to Hangtown. After three full day rides east, they camped near Auburn, still an important Gold Rush boomtown.

"Looks like a good place, Caleb. Nice river here and plenty deadfall for our cooking fire.

"Must be the Bear River, heard it was rich in the Rush. Must be some gold left. Let's use our tin plates tomorrow and see for ourselves."

Two days back and forth, jumping rock to rock to cross, wading the shallow quiet spots before the river gained momentum again on its quest west.

"Nothing on this side, Caleb. But there's a sandy spot just ahead on that quiet curve on left side. Let's try that."

"Got something here and another one, get over here, Diego."

Three days working the stream they had only that one find, and they were pleased with that. They slept that night each with a few tiny nuggets of gold.

"Here's your coffee Caleb, careful the cup's hot."

Finishing a desayuno of pan and dried fruit, Diego and Caleb were debating whether to keep east and cross the mountains using what they reckoned to be the original California trail that early pilgrims had taken to Sutter's Fort or the more leisurely ride south to Hangtown and ride the old Pony Express road, crossing to the east side of the Sierra.

"Don't expect to find any settlements except Nevada City on this old California Trail. The Gold Rush Road will be a lot easier and a bit if history as we ride through those old towns. If I was king, that would be my choice. What say you, cousin?"

"If I were king Caleb the first and last, I'd choose crossing up here keeping on this old road. This is all fresher and wilder. Those old boomtowns will be there, and we can visit them when we get old. Only a week ride from the ranch."

"I bow to you mighty king, we left to search some parts that Jarrett and Noah missed."

CHAPTER TWO

They read the sign NEVADA CITY as they entered town.

"This is a nice old town Caleb, look at those wooden sidewalks and stores for everything,"

"They like their taverns, that's for sure."

"How about a treat and catch an early supper and then camp out of town. There's a bookstore, let's see if they have any maps or info we might use after we eat."

Across the street at Jeanne's, they ate pork chops with applesauce, fried potatoes and beans. Jeanne was born in Nevada City, her parents one of the first to make a claim, a moderate find but enough to set them up in business. Her folks owned two of the taverns, both named The Adler, the restaurant and a boarding house and Jeanne liked to talk about the old days.

"Here's my little tutorial fellas. First, if you don't have a place to put your head down tonight, why not stay at our place? Put you up in a room with two beds for a dollar and then a big breakfast here before you head out in the morning. Nevada City's a fine little town with only a few shootings now and then.

Always been a bit of a history buff, thought folks should know that California was not the first gold rush, that honor belongs to North Carolina fifty years before the Marshall find. A seventeen-pound nugget was discovered which brought thirty thousand people. I wrote a little book on the California pioneers and the Gold Rush; you can buy it across the street at our bookshop."

"Is Adler your last name, Jeanne?"

"It is, you must've read the signs."

After spending the night at the boarding house, breakfast with Jeanne and an hour in her bookshop, they rode out of Nevada City with a promise to return if ever they rode this way again.

"Good time there Diego, the best thing was Jeanne and that little map she sold us. Might help us find our way."

Donner Pass was a barely a trail, winding up a few miles and down halfway, then up again, for three days. The cousins didn't know but they had crossed over Emigrant Gap where those first settlers in the 1840's, only thirty years before, had to lower their wagons and reluctant animals on ropes in order to carry on. All part of the California Trail.

Beat! Their horses weary as well. They looked forward to a little rest before Truckee, their first town since Nevada City.

"Need a wash Diego, that stream looks mighty inviting, some sandy there."

"Right behind you, partner."

They built a small fire, drank coffee and chewed jerky while their clothes dried.

"Never knew what Nevada meant after all these years. Jeanne's booklet here says it's a Spanish word means snowy or covered in snow."

Truckee town was a nice break from the trail.

"I asked around and found a good ol' boy who knows how Truckee got its name."

"How's that Diego?"

"Fella I talked with earlier, been here a long time, said it was a Paiute word. *Tro-kay* was a greeting, meant everything's all right. Before that, Truckee was Colburn Station."

"Like the idea of using Indian names for places that were theirs first."

"Sounds like something Jarrett would say, Diego."

"This trail out of town's better than the one getting here. Should see that lake that talkative man said was just south a day."

Winding through different kinds of pines, Jeffrey, Sugar, Ponderosa, then quaking aspen and white fir for a view of a setting sun glorifying the majesty of Lake Tahoe.

"Look at that azul, maybe the lake Jarrett and Noah talk about. Let's camp here a few days. You have Noah's Henry, find us a deer, Caleb. We'll have venison and dry some for jerky."

"Can afford some days, still early summer. Can't help thinking about those Donner folks. We can take some time to read Jeanne's description of that tragedy. Got my rod. I'll try for some rainbows or whatever trout live here. Remember, when you go for that deer, I'm the one wearing two legs."

With the coals sputtering to a finish and the stars to take their place, they reviewed their days and were satisfied with their progress. They had strung the venison from branches high enough to protect the meat from bears.

"Did Noah ever tell you about his family up there?"

"Si, the first time we went camping."

"Buena here, be nice to stick around and have a good look. Appreciate Jeanne, she's knows some, writes a fine story. Good to know where we are and the names of places. Her map ends here at the top of the lake."

"Noah would be proud of you Caleb. You're a chip off the old block, he's always wanting to know where he is and the names of places."

The next morning, it was Diego's turn to do the breakfast. This morning boiled eggs and dried fruit they'd bought from Jeanne.

"What does Jeanne say about the Donners?"

"Let's see. Here it is, *Delayed by a series of mishaps, they spent the winter of 1846-1847 snowbound in the Sierra Nevada near Truckee.* Goes on and says, *Of the eighty-seven members forty-eight survived, trapped almost four months by the snow. No food for weeks, they resorted to cannibalism eating friends that died of starvation and sicknesses.* She adds that cannibalism might be exaggerated."

"Hate to leave, but the venison is jerked, dry but still chewy."

"Let's find the eastern side of these Sierra Nevada. Maybe find a settlement and fill our saddlebags."

At the bottom of the lake, they met an east-west trail.

"Where do you think this goes, Diego?"

"Maybe this is that Pony Express Road, east all the way to Missouri and west through Hangtown to Sacramento."

"This is the trail we would have taken if we had chosen our first plan."

"At least we can ride it a while, east out of the mountains."

They made camp at dusk.

CHAPTER THREE

Paiutes were the indigenous Americans of the Eastern Sierra Nevada. The first white Sierra explorers to the region were Jedediah Strong Smith, Tom Fitzpatrick and their crew in 1827, followed by Joseph Walker, Kit Carson, John C. Freemont and his soldiers in the 1840's.

Diego and Caleb felt fortunate to experience something of what those first American explorers encountered. Riding down from the mountains on a steep narrow trail they found a town.

Genoa surprised them and pleasantly. Started as a trading post in 1851 on the emigrant Trail, it had grown to a substantial community and county seat when the boys arrived. Genoa, Nevada's first town, was first settled by Mormons.

"That thirst parlor looks like a good place Caleb. What say you, amigo?"

Tying their horses at the far end of the rail they entered through swinging doors. The piano player was trying 'Goodbye Liza Jane'.

At the crowded bar they ordered their beer and were curious that most patrons were fancied up a bit. The barman, Jimmy Delaney, liked to talk between orders.

"Most of the wealth in this valley is account of that Comstock Lode over in Virginia City 'bout thirty miles to the east. Silver don't stop. Discovered back in fifty-nine and still going strong. Seems all those gold rushers rushed over here and a bunch more from back east too. Excuse me, gotta pour some beer.

As I was saying, Virginia City is the wild town, this here is quiet compared, at least most nights. Now and then it gets a bit rowdy. I like it this way, don't have to replace broken glasses very often. You might have a look at Carson City, it's only a day up the road and Reno another two. We've been a state now for fifteen years. Nevada's harsh but plenty rich, oughta stick around fellas, always room for two more."

Diego and Caleb left Genoa and Virginia City to the silver miners and found a trail south, camping some miles outside of town.

"We're on our own now, pard. Hard to get lost with those peaks always on our right. Jimmy Delaney thought the mountains reached all the way to South America, then added he really didn't know. Local knowledge is good, but only for local."

Most days it seemed they forded a stream falling from the hills, crossing each carefully. Jarrett suppling them with trout whenever they wanted.

"How did these fish get up here in the mountains, Diego? Our nuns would tell us, but that seems too simple."

The explorers took a day off to wash their clothes, inspect their tack and groom their mounts. Along a river once visited by Joseph Walker, Diego finished his chores near dusk and found a promising pool to fish for dinner. Returning to camp an hour later, he found a small fire going.

"I do have two fine fish for us but a finer story to share. Don't know if I'll tell it though."

"Why not, cousin?"

"You probably won't believe me."

"Probably not but try me."

"Well, I already had these two beauties but there was a big boy I had been trying for. Was getting dark so I reckoned one last try. As I was drying the fly back and forth before my last cast, a flying fish hit. I was working that flying fish I couldn't see up in the air for at least a couple minutes."

"You're right so far, Diego, does sound like a fish story."

"That flying fish finally got himself tangled in a small pine by the side of the river. You know there's about a yard of leader between the line and the lure, so I took my fingers and followed it up to a couple inches of the hook then rubbed a match on my pants and there he was lit up by the flame. Scary, a bat! I caught a bat! He thought my fly was a real fly. I touched the flame close to the hook and he flew away to hunt again."

"Don't think you could make up a yarn like that, so I believe it's true, especially if you grill those two trout. I'll even clean them."

"Different this east side when you get down from the mountains, kind of stark and treeless. That western side thick with pines this side dramatic jagged peaks. Nice valley here between the Sierra and those dry looking big mountains to the east and lots of good water in these streams for us and our horses. Horses seem fit."

"Those big dry mountains have snow on them Diego and it's July, must be pretty high. This valley would be dry without these streams, they seem to come down out of every canyon."

"Maybe we could drive a herd one of these days over that Pony Express road, this whole valley is well watered. Wonder who owns all this."

"Maybe the Indians."

"The mountains catch all the rain, and all that snowmelt makes this valley green, good cow country."

"Wonder if there's any gold on this side."

"Probably as scarce as the girls, Caleb."

"Sign coming up, Diego. Been 'bout ten days since we left Genoa."
"And a road of sorts east. Been some weather on that sign. BODI 13 miles. Let's have a look. We can be there tomorrow."

The next evening, they could see the tented settlement as they rode. In an hour, they found a tent that forgot it was once white selling whiskey and beans to the two dozen or so miners. After finding water for their horses, they entered.

"Howdy boys, don't see new faces often, welcome to Bodi, don't look to be prospectors, just driftin'?"

"Yes sir, just out to see what's around these parts. Surprised to find this place. You're all by yourselves out here. Appreciate it if you could sell us some of those frijoles, I smell cooking."

"Just about ready and I got some good sourdough to go with it. Fella by the name of W.S. Bodey from Poughkeepsie found some gold hereabouts in fifty-nine and then died in a blizzard the following November. Some of these boys are determined there's a rich lode hereabouts, plenty of promising rock. I gave up and started this little enterprise."

After a cave-in 1875 revealed rich pay dirt, the town grew from a few dozen to nearly 10,000 and thirty-four million dollars were gleaned from her mines. Bodi was a real boomtown and earned her wild west stories. As a bustling gold mining town, Bodi boasted a

Wells Fargo Bank, a post office, four volunteer fire companies, a brass band, a miner's union, several daily papers, a gas station, a jail, and at its peak, sixty-five thirsty saloons on her mile-long Main Street. Murders, shootouts, barroom brawls and stagecoach holdups would make a John Wayne movie proud.

Bodi's several hundred Chinese had a Taoist temple and plentiful opium dens. These Chinese were not allowed to join the miner's union which kept them from high-paying jobs. They sold vegetables, operated laundries and cut and delivered firewood.

By the 1880s, other boomtowns like Tombstone in Arizona lured the quick-rich diggers away and left Bodi to evolve into a community with churches and a schoolhouse. Of course, the gold declined and in 1942, all mines were shut down and Bodi was left to history as a ghost town.

Bodi was too dreary to stay, so the next morning, after some more beans they were off heading south through easy hills and in a few hours another surprise, a huge lake.

"Don't let the horses drink, Diego. This lake's all salty like. Sure funny, all that fresh snowmelt filling this lake. Lots of birds though. They seem to like it."

"They're sea gulls, Diego, thousands of sea gulls."

Two weeks later, the cousins following the Owens River that parallels the Sierra, found Owens Lake named by Freemont in 1845 after one of his guides, Richard Owens. Another saline lake, the Owens collected from the streams flowing from the Sierra into one of the hundred fifty desert basins that form the Great Basin of the United States. Bordered on the east by those dry White Mountains, the lake waited, one day to be denied water. Los Angeles which would also do a job on Mono Lake would take the water before it flowed into both Mono and Owens lakes. Mono Lake and Owens Lake are both saline soda lakes formed when water is collected in terminal basins without an outlet.

Diego and Caleb camped between Mt. Whitney at 14,505 feet above sea level and Bad Water Basin, Death Valley at 279 feet below, only eighty-eight miles apart.

"Let's try one of those flints Jarrett gave us to start a fire. Noah dared us to try and don't know when we'll find a store to buy matches."

After several tries, a good spark, a glow, a few gentle puffs and fire. Two rainbows caught in the river above the lake along with some forgotten root vegetables they found in the saddlebags was dinner. The conversation was dominated with dreamy talk of dessert: churros, tortilla española, sopaipillas and flan.

During 1862 and 1863, the Owens Valley War was fought between the original Paiutes and California Volunteers and local settlers. Minor hostilities continued occasionally until 1867.

The Sierra diminished as they continued south, another mountain range appearing in the haze to take its place, basin and range over and over.

"What the hell are those, Diego?"

"Sister Marie Louise showed us pictures when we studied Egypt."

"Camels, cousin. They're camels! We've come a far piece, but don't think we're in Egypt."

The United States Army experimented in California with camels as pack animals and they proved to be hardy and well suited to the southwest. The Civil War intervened, and the experiment was abandoned. Most camels were sold at auction but a few escaped or let loose to roam.

Finding some shade, they halted for the day.

"Sierra don't seem to go all the way to South America, Diego. Mountains quit on us. Other mountains up ahead. Can't wait too long to choose a way, water's going to be a problem."

They knew the west side was greener with more options for water. Crossing over, they found a river and followed it through the mountains, then a difficult winding trail of sorts through foothills to the central valley and headed south again.

The last few days had been a nice easy route, except for the steep winding decent. The boys had found the Kern River and crossed between present day Mojave and Bakersfield.

The next dawn, they rode south a few days exploring their new options.

"More hazy mountains ahead Diego, don't look so rugged. Let's find some water if we can and stop for a coffee and talk."

They didn't find water, so they walked with their horses.

"If I was by myself Caleb, I'd try that pass twisting like one of Miguel's grapevines."

"Good as any Diego, let's go see."

"Looks like an old army post ahead Caleb, deserted for a while by the looks of things, let's check it out. Might find some water in that old well over there."

Fort Tejon had been intermittently active from 1854 until 1864. Located between the San Emigdio and Tehachapi Mountains, the fort was the terminus of the U.S. Camel Corps.

"This wheel, am I pushing or am I pulling?"

"Think maybe both, but are you bringing any agua?"

"Si, and it smells fresh."

After inspecting the abandoned buildings, they rode the hills and spotted antelope, elk and deer as well as all sorts of birds, condors rode the wind as the boys rode the hills.

"Don't know where this trail goes. Seems a natural route, still going south by the looks of the shadows. Been noticing all the slants in the rocks for the last few days, all those angles. Don't seem natural. Think maybe earthquakes worked on these boys."

"Let's hope they rest while we're riding through."

CHAPTER FOUR

In a week the trail gentled into the valley and the cousins found the pueblo. The population had grown to nearly six thousand.

"The City of the Angels seems slow, not a bad way to live. Think we should find a stable. Need to stretch these legs of mine and towns sometimes hard to get around with caballos."

"No problemo with walking, primo."

Camping on the river a mile north of town, the cousins secured their goods and walked to Olvera Street, the old Spanish settlement. They felt contento as the beers arrived almost cold.

"That's about it for dinero, time for trabajo."

"Might be good for a while yet without working."

"How's that, Diego.?"

"Before we left, Jarrett gave me something."

Reaching into his 'Vaquero Style' pants, tight waisted with loose-fitting bottoms, he ceremoniously placed the coin on the table.

"That's gold Diego, this is a twenty-dollar Liberty."

"It is, and it's ours."

Their personal gold rush needed to be celebrated with a few more cervezas at ten cents per glass. Besides the Liberty, they tallied the rest of their stash: four half-cents, seven one-cent, two five-cent and four seated Liberty fifty-cent pieces.

"Look across the street, right on Main, that beautiful big building. Says Pico House on the sign. Must be three stories high and new. That's going to last a long time, be nice to stay there someday."

"Don't think an earthquake can bring that one down."

In the morning after a quick coffee and some dried fruit, they walked to the stables, got directions then rode the ten miles to the Rancho La Brea Tar Pits. One of the Olvera Street regulars had told them about this strange place.

"Be careful here, don't want this goo all over our boots. Or get stuck."

"Looks like some sort of bones sticking out over here. Wonder what's under us?"

The asphalt seeps had been used by Native Americans as a glue and caulk and early Angelenos as a roofing material. The Death Trap of the Ages was only a curiosity until 1908 and only then studied seriously by paleontologists.

Twenty-six miles south, they found work as stevedores unloading and loading the few ships that visited the small bay at San Pedro. Their wages took care of their necessities. They used an abandoned shed for shelter and a bathroom at the port. Their horses were kept by a farmer two miles away who traded the boarding for fertilizer.

The Spanish crown in 1784 awarded seventy-five thousand acres to a soldier, Juan Jose Dominguez and his descendants. His rancho becoming the cities of San Pedro, Palos Verde, Redondo Beach, Hermosa Beach east to the Los Angeles River, including the cities of Lomita, Gardena, Harbor City, Wilmington, Carson, Compton, and western portions of Long Beach and Paramount. The rancho's economy was based on tallow and hides.

Descendant Manuel Rodriguez, at twenty-nine, was elected mayor of Los Angeles.

Rancho owners found it impossible to prove their legal rights under American law, even though the Treaty of Guadalupe Hidalgo assured their claims would be honored. This was now white California! Over and over again, portions of their land were sold to pay legal fees and travel to the San Francisco courts was a difficult journey in those early days, land-rich and cash-poor.

The huge Spanish land grants were eventually divided among powerful Anglo families who prospered dividing their holdings with real estate deals.

Of course, the Native Americans, over one-hundred different tribes that were quilted between coast, valley, foothill, and desert had no courts to protect their rights from the Spanish, the Mexicans and now the Anglos.

On their days off, the boys visited the mission San Gabriel and camped on the San Gabriel River next to Governor Pio Pico's hacienda.

All this wonderment under the dominion of the San Gabriel and San Bernardino Mountains, mantled with snow in the winters.

When Diego and Caleb weren't working or exploring, they challenged the surf. Diego with his fly rod was learning the difference between freshwater trout and the mysteries of the sea. Diego found sport shops selling fishing equipment and bought stronger leader material and ocean lures. Taking advantage of San Pedro's cheap cantinas, they whiled away some time.

"What do you think, Diego?"

"Spinning wheels for three months now."

"You ready to find something new?"

"Ready, let's finish our job with the ship here and we'll give notice."

"Our horses are stout, and we have fodder for scant times. The Henry's oiled and clean, saddle bags full of staples and matches dipped in wax in case they get wet. What do you have, Diego?"

"Plenty dried fish, chiles, frijoles, fruit, nuts and coffee. One pot and that grill you made will make cooking easier."

"Should have learned to use a slingshot. Worked for Jarrett and Noah. Let's see here, yup here's my poncho and slicker for rain, got yours?"

The cousins were free as the breeze and they did as they pleased, away from home six months.

"Where we headed?"

"If I'm still king, I'd try for San Diego."

"I'll join you, your majesty."

Saying adios to the other Mexicans they'd been spending off time with, the cousins followed the sea south, camping on la playa.

After visiting the Mission San Juan Capistrano, they finished their dinner and chores and talked around their small fire.

"Miss the stars, Diego. Half the nights here there's this cloud cover, leaves before noon but returns hiding those special stars. Like to think on those patterns Jarrett and Noah pointed out when we camped. Made friends with that Ursa Major and his little brother, Ursa Minor, always there if it's clear."

"Can always find the North Star, Polaris. It's the tip of the handle of the Little Dipper and just off the spout of the Big Dipper. That's our guiding star. Know all this Caleb, something we grew up with."

"We won't need any stars for a guide as long as we have this ocean. Ever think about who lives way over there, Chinese and Japanese anyway. Or why the folks who live on the bottom don't fall off. Sister Maria whacked my hand once for spelling gravity with an 'f'. Funny, it hurt at the time but now I remember it and it makes me kinda proud."

With the year 1870 a few months away, they both slept with the musica del mar.

CHAPTER FIVE

Riding for San Diego, Caleb was wondering aloud about the old mission buildings they called on in San Juan Capistrano.

"Earthquakes have damaged them some, then they fix them up and hope for the best."

"Got to wondering myself."

"What got your attention this morning, mi primo."

"Whether I'm a Mexican, a Spaniard, an Anglo, or a Latino, a Mestizo, or a Chicano. Chicano I guess."

"I decided a long time ago about me."

"So, what are you besides a cousin?"

"Well first I'm an American."

"And second?"

"And second I'm an American, pretty simple to me. I know the difference but don't choose to dwell on it."

"That's why you're King Caleb l."

Fishing from the surf, Diego provided a corvina for the grill. Caleb added half a jalapeño and a pasillo pepper. A week more riding to San Diego with the playa, the sun and the surf was too pleasant to hurry. They looked forward to returning the same way.

"Been good to have a settlement now and then, have some cervezas and maybe meet some girls."

Twice each day they rode inland two hundred yards for their horses to graze. When they caught sight of the settlement, they continued directly for the mission. Jarrett and Noah had shared with them stories about their amigo, Sebastion. All they knew was that he had a small cantina and was the librarian of the Mission San Diego.

And there at the mission library they found Sebastion, a generation later. "Señores, may I help?"

"Señor Sebastion? This is my primo Caleb, I am Diego, we're

sons of old amigos, Jarrett and Noah Andersen. They visited with you maybe twenty years ago. We had to see you and explain how rico they were for having known you."

"Por favor sit, some café and we talk. I am Sebastion, Señor Sebastion was my father. Diego, you have the same name as our namesake, San Diego. Do you know about Diego, Diego?"

"I don't, all I've ever known is that Diego is a similar name to Jaime and Santiago, James in English."

"There is some confusion over our Diego who was actually Diego de San Nicholas del Puerto. Pope Sixtus gave him the holy name Didecus. The rest we'll leave to the cardinals in Rome to debate and decide."

One hour passed and a half more. "Bueno, now follow me please to our cellar y poco vinto tino and a little celebrate."

Sebastion insisted they sleep at the mission. An Indio collected their horses. The teacher and students spent two days talking about old Californio.

"¿Donde ahora, amigos?"

"El Norte, we hope to see more of Californio. We learned from our fathers and they learned from you, Sebastion. Historia y cultura es muy importante but first we need to see su pueblo and then some trabajo."

Sebastion helped them get jobs at the port where they worked for a month on the fishing boats, saving enough to supply them for their next leg.

Riding north from San Diego, they felt richer for their experiences and would keep warm memories of Sebastion.

"¿Donde?"

"Let's go see what we wanted to see from the start."

"The Gold Road it is. Wonder how you get there?"

"We can always follow our path to Los Angeles and then all the way to back to Genoa, find that Pony Express Road west to Hang Town."

"Nah. Done that."

"Then let's head up the coast to Monterrey and ask some questions. Must have nice playas and maybe some towns on the way."

"And the ocean's our guide."

Six weeks later, they rode into Monterrey.

On a whim, they celebrated the new year of 1871 tardily at Segovia's Tavern by the lighthouse. Cowboys from a ranch east of town a few miles were drinking with other hands from a neighboring ranch.

Explaining to the ranch hands that they were celebrating New Year's Eve a month later, the cowboys enthusiastically joined the party. After midnight sometime, somebody spilled a drink on somebody and somebody threw their beer on somebody and somebody punched somebody. And somebody turned into everybody.

When it was finished Diego had a split lip, a loose tooth and a bitten ear. Caleb a black eye and sore ribs. As the sun was rising, they followed the cowboys to their ranch.

Rancho Colinas was a substantial holding in gentle hills east some miles of Monterrey. No sleep for the rowdy. The cowboys worked the day. Juan O' Brennan, the foreman, realized his men had been on a hoot but that was their choice. He still expected a day's work.

Diego and Caleb rode with the cowboys staying out of their way. Ross Bauer, an older hand, introduced them to Mr. O' Brennan at the end of the day. O' Brennan had been observing, watching them ride and appreciating their interest. He hired them at twenty-five dollars for each month working the ranch. Ross showed them the bunkhouse and the privy. Meals were substantial and simple. Hogs and chickens were kept as well as the cattle.

"To be honest with you Mr. O' Brennan, we don't know much about cattle, our families grow grapes for wine in Sonoma. But we know horses and how to work hard."

"Fair enough, the fellas will show you how things are done.

Ross will get you started. They're all yours, Ross."

"Follow along boys, we'll ride over to the corral and get you started."

"Cattle's just a general name for these beeves. The Colinas run Hereford. Your jobs will be roping, castrating and branding after roundup next week. Your timing is good, we always can use extra hands.

Folks call 'em cows but there are different kinds of cows. A cow is a female bovine who has birthed at least one calf. A heifer is a female of one or two years who has yet to be bred. You can see over to your left, the heavier ones are the cows. Heifers don't have udders yet."

"Got that, Ross."

"Gotta keep some bulls for breeding, they're the ones with the cajones. If we didn't castrate most of 'em it would be hell out there, all the bulls fighting like buffalo. They're the ones to keep an eye on, can be dangerous. Bulls have the bigger shoulders, can grow to eighteen hundred pounds. I see you boys ride geldings, same story with horses.

"Then a steer must be a castrated bull."

"Correct, they grow fatter and are better for meat. You know what oxen are?"

"Know they hauled folks out west."

"Correct, oxen are draft animals and have been around for twice as long as Jesus. Some places they call 'em bullocks. They're larger breeds used for the big jobs. We don't keep 'em on our spread. You'll probably see a few Longhorn in the hills though. Keep some as a reminder of the ol' days, but no bulls, those ol' boys can really be salty."

A week later, Ross who had taken Diego and Caleb under a paternal wing asked, "Did you ever hear 'bout the old California bull fights? Spaniards and Mexicans used to fight bulls regular like against each other but now and then some vaquero would trap a grizzly and the bear would fight a bull on Sunday."

"Who won those fights?"

"Don't rightly know, Diego. Who would you guess?"

"Think maybe the bull."

"Really brutal, a throwback to Roman times."

"Another messy entertainment is cock fightin', you can find 'em on Sundays usually on the edge of town. A real blood sport where the roosters are bred to fight and kill. Build a pit where they fight, lots of money bet, really passionate. Don't watch 'em myself."

Diego and Caleb worked three months on the Colinas ranch. On their days off they rode the hills, Diego trying for trout and steelhead in the Salinas River north of Monterrey. This spring the hills were on fire with wildflowers: lupine, purple owl's clover, phacelia, Indian paintbrush, buttercups and the California poppy over and over again. They left Segovia's Tavern on Saturday nights to the cowboys.

"What do you think, mighty king?"

"Well my most loyal subject, I think it's time to scratch the itch.

It's always hard to adios a place that's been good to us. We've made friends but we gotta leave sometime, cousin."

"The roundup's been finished a month. Seems quiet on Colinas, how 'bout we tell Ross and Mr. O' Brennan after dinner Sunday. We can thank the hands as well."

Explaining to Mr. O' Brennan their goal was to explore California, Caleb then asked how come he had an Irish name being Mexican and all.

"Good question, Caleb. During the Mexican War, my father was an Irish immigrant living in New York. He joined the army and was assigned to a company of Irish soldiers. While in Mexico, they deserted and joined the Mexicans who they believed were more like them, Catholic and all that. Called themselves the St. Patrick Battalion. About two hundred, real heroes in Mexico."

"What happened to them, Mr. O' Brennan?"

"After the Battle of Churubusco which the Mexicans fought fiercely, they were captured and hung as traitors. Luckily for me, my father Michael escaped, married my mother and here I am. We Irish have a saying, 'What's for ya won't pass ya."

The next morning, Mr. O' Brennan, Ross and the hands, saluting with their hats waved them on.

CHAPTER SIX

Molly and Adalyn in swimming costumes, showing a rumor of leg but hinting more, greeted the boys as they rode their mounts zigging and zagging the shallow surf as it advanced and retreated.

"Howdy ladies."

"Well howdy to you, cowboys."

With a pleasant back and forth they tipped their flat-crowned sombreros and dismounted.

"You lose some cows, haven't seen many on the beach and we've been here all day", Molly teased.

"My cousin Diego and I rounded them up a while back and are looking for stray heifers. Any of you fine ladies a stray? Name's Caleb. Where are we? Been riding a few days since Monterrey."

"Santa Cruz, cowboys. We were just to brave the surf, climb on down and join us. Oh, I'm Molly and my friend here is Adalyn, Addy."

"Be nice, but we've nothing to swim in."

"Well Caleb, you have your birthday suit and we won't peek."

"Maybe a little", from Addy.

And they did.

In the late afternoon, Diego caught a halibut off the surf while Caleb rode a mile into Santa Cruz for a jug of wine.

Building a small fire on the beach they grilled the fish, added their chiles and drank vino tinto from California's first winery, the Buena Vista.

"Lots of wines made in Sonoma, that's where Diego and I live."

Molly, the most curious asked, "What did you do, I mean did you go to school up there?"

"No schools there yet, the nuns taught us. Our folks have a ranch and we grow the grapes that make this wine. Thinking about maybe starting our own winery."

"Think there's more to our cowboys that what we first thought, Molly."

As the fire dimmed, Caleb and Addy drifted off to the girls' cabin, just off the beach.

Diego spread the blankets and told Molly about his stars.

Later, with the eastern sky warning of dawn, "You taste salty, Molly."

"You as well Diego, good salty."

"Didn't know you were so religious, Mol."

Molly stretching on their blankets asked, "Why do you say that, Diego?"

"You yelled for God a few times last night."

"Glad you can't see me blush. What say we go to church again?" And they did.

Molly and Adalyn were coeds at Leland Stanford Junior University. It was Easter break, a week away from their books.

Caleb and Addy were sharing a pot of coffee.

"How do you two get back and forth between Santa Cruz and Palo Alto. Didn't see any horses."

There's a Butterfield Overland Mail stagecoach between Santa Cruz and Palo Alto towns, its forty-five miles, takes a day. Then the stage finishes in San Jose."

"What's your favorite classes, Addy?"

"Math and physics, in my third year studying engineering, civil engineering, I'm the only female in my classes."

"What kind of an engineer is a civil engineer, does that mean you're a nice lady that drives a train?"

"Don't be so corny, Caleb. That's you, my 'Corny Caleb'.

Seriously, there was that Emperor Norton years back in San Francisco with all that talk about building tunnels under The City and a bridge spanning San Francisco with Oakland."

"Heard about him, a kook but fun."

"Don't think his ideas were so crazy. His idea is going to be my senior thesis. There's this architectural student who I'm teaming with and we're going to build a bridge, a San Francisco Bridge across the bay all the way to Oakland, at least on paper with models."

Back at the beach with easy talk, Molly asked if they had ever watched a game of rugby football.

"Haven't but heard there's lots of running with a ball and tackling, pretty rough sport."

"Addy and I have an idea. Next November, Stanford and Cal are playing, big rivals. This year's games at The Farm, that's our name for Stanford. Why don't you figure a way to come by Palo Alto.

We can all go to the game and to the party after, that's even more fun. You can meet our friends and we'll show you around the campus."

Molly added, "Stanford's mascot is the Indian and you're the cowboys. We'll be the cowboys and Indians."

"A fine idea, what ya' think Caleb, it'll add to our culture which needs a lot of adding to. Have to stable our horses and find a place to stay."

"And some new clothes, don't want to embarrass our ladies."

"You're fine the way you are, you're our cowboy vaqueros, remember? Stanford has all different kinds of students and faculty from all over. Might not even notice you."

"Oh, the girls will Addy, we'll have to keep these two to ourselves. Think they could stay in one of the dorms?"

"I think we might find something better than that, Molly. We could find a place for the four of us off campus and make it much more than a rugby game."

"That's seven months away, will you two even remember us?"

"Vaqueros never forget beautiful ladies, so muy simpatica."

"Our very own vaqueros."

At the end of the week, it was time for the carefree girls to return as serious scholars.

"Diego and I have talked it over, we don't want to lose you. We'll find you a week before the Big Game, a promise. Don't you forget us. One question, how can we find you?"

"It's a small campus in Palo Alto, ask anyone and they'll direct you to Admissions. Ask for Smith and Jones. Just kidding ask for Forge or McWhinney, bet you can guess who's McWhinney."

Waving sombreros above their heads, con muchisimo mucho, they were back on their expedition riding east, hoping for a boomtown.

"Did Molly tell you what she's studying, Diego."

"Did. History, she's going to graduate a historian."

"Wonder, what kind of jobs for historians?"

"She said that she could always teach, hopefully at a university. Said most towns and cities expected their female teachers to remain single. Signed contracts that promised they would stay home at night, stuff like that."

"What's the problem with married teachers?"

"Sex my cousin, sex. Married women and all that, don't want their youngsters contaminated, pretty stupid."

"Our nuns never have that problem."

"Verdad."

Riding through Pacheco Pass in the Coastal Mountains, they sighted California's large central valley. Their instincts suggesting their goal was ahead to the east. Trusting their intuition and with water bags filled, they rode slowly on and in a week the foothills.

"Must be the start of the Sierra pard, this western side is mostly gentle and there's a settlement ahead."

"Our star stays true, amigo."

"Verdad."

Mariposa was named after the incredible numbers of butterflies that Gabriel Moraga's expedition encountered in 1806 and was later granted to John C. Freemont. The Gold Rush had overwhelmed the small town, the southernmost in the gold chain with the hopeful and desperate.

"This is the California that Jarrett and Noah talk about, they always said this is where the state's history *officially* started with the rush of the 49ers. Always reminded us that the Indios, Spanish and Mexicans, even the Russians were here first."

Mariposa bragged four thousand five hundred miners, businessmen, gamblers and filles de joire. The boy's idea was to investigate for a day or two.

Helping an old timer catch his horse that had loosed itself from a railing, they accepted his offer of beer at The Diggings.

"Don't mind me, fellas, I'm a bit curious what you two are up to, don't look like no miners, look like vaqueros. No cows in Mariposa except the ones that are barbequed."

"We're tourists, wanting to see California, that's about it."

"You're no city dudes, know that much."

"Live in Sonoma, taking a year or two before we settle."

"Three more cervezas, Arturo." Arturo Lopez had been a miner with enough sense to realize that steady profits would continue as a businessman, without freezing in cold Sierra streams.

"If you're seeing the sights, I got one for you, ever hear of Yosemite?"

"Have, our dads speak about it with a reverence."

"As they should."

"If you have ten days to spare, I'll show it to ya."

"I'd like that, you, Diego?"

"Si. I'm ready when you are. Guess we should meet officially, this is my cousin Diego, I'm Caleb, mucho gusto."

"I'm Cole Keliher, take me a day to get my goods together. Meet you right here tomorrow after the sun comes up."

Riding their horses three days, they climbed gently, thirty-five miles through the forest following the Merced River. Cole raised a hand to halt.

"Okay, fellas, she's gonna show herself soon. A little more, THERE! It's summer and the waterfalls slow a bit. Gotta see it in the spring sometime. Back there over your shoulder is a fall that looks afire, certain time of the day. Now we'll ride down to the valley, 'bout 4,000 feet down there."

Cole showed them the valley of waterfalls and granite for a day, then they rode three days to the grove of Sequoias. Around their fires Cole reminisced, explaining how John Muir had done so much to make people aware and respectful of the mountains.

"Wonder if that could that have been the John that showed our dads Yosemite?"

"Might have been, probably was. If your dads met John Muir, that would have been an honor. He's still very active, spends most of his time in Frisco from what I read. You know about Senator Freemont, his ranch is all 'round Mariposa but it's his wife, Jessie Benton who's working so darn hard to preserve Yosemite from logging, overgrazing, trapping and just darn over developing this place. She's a hard-headed, get things done kinda woman, just what this valley needs. Oughta name a mountain after her. Leave it to the bloodsuckers and this would all look like downtown Mariposa."

Ten days later they were back at The Diggings for beers. The cousins picked their new friend's brain.

"What do you think California will be like in fifty years, Cole?"

"Well now, that's a good question. I've thought on that some. As long as California has sun, it'll do good. But that's also the problem. 'Feard California's gonna get too popular, people from all over coming here. And now we got the railroad to bring 'em. Gold's gonna run out sometime. Cattle and farming's my guess. But can't grow corn on the beaches or grow wheat on top the mountains or potatoes in the deserts and we got plenty of them. If the folks keep coming, don't know, that'll be a problem for the next generations. With the gold gone, what will take its place?"

"It's been a special time for us, Cole. We've been on the road over a year now, this is a perfect halfway celebration."

"Where to now, fellas?"

"Diego and I will wander the boomtowns, maybe as far as Auburn. We have a rugby game to watch in Palo Alto this November. That's the only thing we have to do."

To ward off further commercial exploitation, conservationists convinced President Lincoln to declare Yosemite Valley and the Mariposa Grove of giant sequoias a public trust, the first time the federal government protected land and laid the foundation for the establishment of state and national park systems. Yellowstone became the first national park in 1872, Yosemite and Sequoia in 1890.

Riding north the next morning, they took two weeks investigating Jamestown, Murphys New Diggings, Columbia, Georgetown, El Dorado, Placerville, Sonora and Coloma, the birthplace of the '49er. Of all the boomtowns, Angels Camp was the most entertaining.

Angels Camp, named for its first storekeeper, Henry Angell, was jump started by the Gold Rush but inspired by a frog. Mark Twain put the town and Calaveras County on the history map. Twain heard a story about a man who boasted in a saloon that his frog could jump further than the others. The braggard secured his bet by filling his competitor's frog with buckshot. The tale inspired Twain to write, using colorful local vernacular, *The Celebrated Jumping Frog of Calaveras County*. It was Samuel Clemens first use of his pen name. The Calaveras County Fair still hosts a four-day frog jumping competition on the third weekend of May. Currently the record, set in 1986 by 'Rosie the Ribiter' is nearly twenty-two feet.

Angels Camp's gross recovery of gold until 1910 was twenty million dollars and Angels Creek ran chalky white from the mill waste.

The largest nugget ever found in California weighed one hundred-nine pounds. It was discovered in Sierra Buttes, August 1869. The largest gold nugget ever dug was the Welcome Stranger in Moliagui, Victoria, Australia, also in 1869, weighing one hundred seventy-three pounds.

Needing work again, the cousins investigated logging. There was definitely a demand for timber in the mines of the still-growing boomtowns and the building of the railroads. However, they were upset with the unregulated slaughter, nearly a third of the Sierra Nevada was logged. Concern for the forests led to the creation of state and national parks, but not until the turn of the century.

Disappointed with forestry, Diego and Caleb decided to try the ranchos, this time with experience. With so many vaqueros working the mines, they hired on at twenty-five dollars a month.

CHAPTER SEVEN

The Anglos, who had mostly taken over the ranchos, were now selling beeves to hungry miners. Cattle had reached an astronomical price of fifty-five dollars for an eight hundred fifty-pound steer.

"Been here a month now, Diego and it's la buena vida again. Couldn't do this forever but for now it works."

"Think when you go home, you'll stay home?"

"Might, but ever since we met Molly and Addy I've been thinking of school. Problem is I don't know what I want to do, unless it's just to learn. Seems a waste to spend those years in college and then go home and make wine."

"I know what Noah would say."

"What's that, Caleb?"

"Knowing stuff is never a waste."

"Anyway Diego, what's the hurry? We're only eighteen and fortunate. If we lived in the city with folks that worked regular jobs, we'd be right there working some job or another. They've been working since the age of eleven or twelve. Maybe younger, seventy hours a week."

"I'm interested in most everything but have no passion for anything, unless it's traveling around California."

"Keep working on it, I'll check back with you now and then. In the meantime, we have a problem."

Rustlers had been known to run off with a head or two but here two hombres were stealing a dozen.

"Ride around and make some noise Diego, turn them towards me. Maybe I can scare them off with my Henry. Some cover here."

Waiting till the thieves were even with him, twenty yards between, Caleb started shooting trying to separate the cattle from the crooks. Surprised by the noise, one of the horses reared and threw the rider.

The other bandit when trying to help his partner on his own horse was whacked by Diego with his coiled lariat.

"What are we gonna do with these hombres?"

"I say hang 'em from that oak."

"Too much work, I say we just shoot 'em."

"Do what ya' gotta do mister," from bandit one."

"Me and my brother got nothin' to live for anyways," from bandit two."

"Ever try working."

"Working's for suckers."

"What did rustling get you?"

"Got me there, Mister."

"Diego let's string 'em up here. That'll be five we've hung this month."

"That's what this lariat's for, a nice slow strangle, it'll be fun to watch these two hombres dance, takes 'bout five minutes."

The boys were brave but sweating, fear staring to replace bravado.

"Lemme shoot 'em in the feet first."

"Nah, save your lead for the next one who tries rustlin'."

"Any last words?"

"Reckon I do, I'm the older, dumber brother. Sorry kid. Okay do it."

Diego and Caleb had played their bluff as long as they could.

"If you had a choice, would you trade a hanging for a job on the ranch?"

"Would," from both.

The brothers worked ten years on the ranch before buying a small place of their own.

CHAPTER EIGHT

After riding a week west to San Jose, and stabling their horses, they bought more fitting clothes, with advice from a haberdasher. Their regular outfits they had cleaned and put away in their saddlebags. Finding a barber shop and a bath two blocks away on Market Street took care of that chore. They had saved all their money from months of ranch work. Together they sported two hundred dollars.

San Jose State, the oldest public university on the west Coast was established in 1857. Diego and Caleb were free to walk the campus, admiring Tower Hall covered in ivy. The college was originally a Normal School which prepared teachers.

"Maybe that's what I could do, teach."

"I can't see you Diego, teaching little kids their letters, just doesn't fit a vaquero."

"Was thinking older kids, maybe high school. School only goes on for a hundred thirty days or so, I could teach, then work on our ranch."

"Well you'd be good at lassoing kids that got loose."

"Seriously Caleb, I'm going in and ask at that Administration Office."

A half-hour later Diego returned.

"Look a little dejected Diego."

"When the lady told me that as a high school teacher my pay would probably be room and board, I lost interest."

"How many years would it take?"

"Didn't even bother to ask."

Saddling up, they were off to Palo Alto and Stanford University. After stabling their horses, they found entrepreneurial teenagers selling rides with a rickshaw-bicycle like contraptions.

"Here's the Administration Building Caleb, I'll go ask about Forge and McWhinney."

Twenty minutes later, Diego returned with a smile.

A very nice lady told me they were off campus and gave me these directions. She had instructions to give this address only to Molly McWhinney's older brother, and that's me Diego McWhinney. I fit the description Molly left."

Knocking on the door to the cottage, the girls greeted them coolly.

"No thank you, we don't need anything, maybe the lady across the street" and closed the door, but only partway because Caleb's shined boot was in the way.

"We have a new and improved product to sell you and its free if your nice."

The door opening wide, the girl's smiles wider.

"What happened to Diego and Caleb, we didn't invite pretty school-boys."

"We had to clean up some and reckoned new clothes and a wash might help us meet some pretty girls and here you are. We got a lot to learn and your good teachers, just need a bit of practice."

"Addy and I think you need mucho practice, amigos."

They spent the week touring the campus, attending the parties and at night they made love.

The Big Game on Saturday was well-attended. The game was played on a grass pitch, fifteen players to a side. Stanford won the match thirteen to six. At the post game party both sides were bruised, some bloodied, all smiling and sharing beers. A sign outside read, *Soccer is a gentleman's game played by ruffians, and rugby is a ruffian's game played by gentlemen.*

Back with Molly and Addy, Diego and Caleb were excited. "That's the best fun I've ever had."

"You are mean, Diego, I thought maybe I was a little more fun than that old football game."

"You are my love, you are," and they retired to their room. Addy and Caleb talked and more the whole night long.

Monday rolled around as it always does after Sunday. Molly and Addy had classes to attend.

"Still going to build that bridge across the bay, Caleb. My partner and I have three months left to present our thesis. And classes start at ten for me."

"We'll talk tonight, Addy, go build your bridge."

When the girls left, they made another pot of coffee and talked things over.

"Think we'll be a distraction to the girls if we stay, Diego."

"Know they'll be a distraction to me."

"What's your feelings for Molly, Diego?"

"She's special Caleb, my first true love. But we don't have much in common. Molly's going to teach, probably at a college. She's talking about a master's degree which takes another year after regular graduation. Hate to just leave with a 'thank you ma'am' but can't just hang around while she goes to school. Think it best if I ride on. What's your thoughts, cousin?"

"Same, Caleb. I have strong feelings for Addy, but she'll build bridges and tunnels, and I'll probably grow grapes and make wine."

"Let's leave tomorrow after proper goodbyes, Molly and Addy know where we live."

And they did the next morning.

Riding north along the coast, Caleb asked how many names he had,

"The last time I counted I had four, two last names, Andersen from dad and Contreras from mom, then Diego and Raul. You can call me Diego Raul Andersen Contreras if you have the time. Think our abeuelos have more than that, tradition goes back to Spain."

"Same with me, you know our dads don't even have a middle name. Different cultures."

CHAPTER NINE

San Francisco was a natural destination, just up the peninsula thirty-three miles, the cousins quiet on their ride.

"There's the bay where Molly's will build her bridge, would be something to see. Do you think it can be done?"

"Heard our dads talking awhile back and one of them said that if you can think it you can do it."

After stabling their horses on the edge of The City, they rode public conveyances around, first finding a small hotel, then Fisherman's Wharf for shellfish. They had one hundred fifty dollars between them. Young hoodlums were patrolling their turf making mischief, assaulting folks and making nuisances of themselves. They stayed clear of Diego and Caleb who had developed a certain confidence.

Buying a newspaper to find what might be going on, Caleb read aloud, "John Muir, noted conservationist speaking tonight at City Hall."

"Have to go, primo, maybe he'd take time to talk with us about Jarrett and Noah."

Nearly seventy seated themselves in the auditorium and listened as a bearded Muir explained the condition of the Sierra with the destruction that mining had brought, the wasting of the mountains, deforestation and polluted streams. Without meaningful regulation, greed would keep destroying what God and Mother Nature had taken millions of years to give, this Gift of the Mountains. Muir was passionate and persuasive to people without power. He suggested a club of sorts, that maybe with education more folks would join their quest, not to stop the miners, but regulate them with sensible measures to slow down and then end the destruction. Then he talked about the beauty of Yosemite and the need to protect it.

After his presentation, Muir generously chatted with his admirers and a few newspapermen. Last in line, Caleb introduced themselves. Muir, stroking his beard suggested they take a seat.

"Jarrett and Noah, I do remember. Those two young fellas were excited as any I've shown the valley to. I was sheepherding those days. We camped almost two weeks together. Maybe they'll join the new club we're starting. What are those two up to nowadays?"

"They had a high adventure in China, made some money and bought a ranch in Sonoma where they grow grapes. What are you going to call your new group, Mr. Muir?"

"Call me John, fellas. Decided to name it the Sierra Club." Trying to be guardians, that simple. But we need powerful advocates like The Big Four but their way too busy making their fortunes."

The next night they tried the Tadich Grill of which their dads had talked. When the waiter asked what they wanted, Diego asked him whatever he suggested, within reason.

The experienced and observant server suggested starting with a citrussy white wine, a Spanish Rioja Godello. The boys were now in their own territory and Diego countered with, "A nice California Sauvignon Blanc, please."

The waiter brought them clam chowders and shrimp and crab salads with a creamy dill dressing, finishing with bread puddings.

"Heard that name Big Four a few times, got me curious."

"How about we find the library tomorrow and find out."

The public library on Larkin Street provided the answers.

Overwhelmed with all the information, they asked the librarian, a strong, no-nonsense looking Miss Judith Davis if there might be a simpler publication about The Big Four.

Miss Davis found them what they needed, four individual simplified biographies. They asked Miss Davis and received library cards. Using their hotel address, they checked out the pamphlets then rode a carriage to Golden Gate Park that had recently opened in 1870.

Paying the driver, they found a generous tree offering shade. Built on San Francisco sand dunes, the park had occasional bison roaming the thousand-acre park.

"Here's a man we almost know Diego, Amasa Leland Stanford. He was an industrialist and politician who made his money as a storekeeper during the Gold Rush. Seems like the big money he made was from selling the 49ers their goods. Was a governor of California, a U.S. Senator and railroad president of the Central Pacific and later the Southern Pacific. Oh oh, here's a footnote, says he's widely considered a robber baron, can only guess what that means. Did start the university, named it after his son."

"Very concise report, primo. This Collis Potter Huntington fella, same general story, invested in an idea that a Theodore Judah had of building the Central Pacific Railroad as part of the transcontinental railroad. Then he went on developing a couple others, the Southern Pacific and the Chesapeake and Ohio Railway. Your turn Caleb."

"Okay, Mark Hopkins joined our heroes, investing in the railroads then concentrated on hotels, says he's worth forty million. He's about sixty and prefers to be known as one of the Associates rather than one of The Big Four."

"That leaves a Caleb Andersen, worth maybe fifty dollars. Goes on and says he built a trail between Sonoma and Napa, a real big shot!"

"Now we have The Big Five, How about that?"

"The last guy's Charles Crocker. Not much different here, one of the founders of the Central Pacific, then more about, let's see, then took control of the Southern Pacific. He's worth twenty million and says he's a Republican. Has six kids. Wonder if they have to do the dishes? At the end here, says they are philanthropists supporting favorite charities."

"Just remembered our nuns teaching us American History said that John Pierpont Morgan, a banker in the Gilded Age was maybe the richest man in America, saying something like, saving money is like saving dead fish."

"And remember they taught us that Andrew Carnegie was the richest man in the world and gave it all away building libraries. Bet they would have helped Mr. Muir."

On the way back to their hotel, they stopped again at Fisherman's Wharf less than five miles from the park. They ate a seafood grill and drank an ale and a porter crafted by the Mission Street Brewery. Caleb mentioned the Transcontinental Railroad of which he had just read to the barman. Mike Sweeney knew a lot about a lot and happened to be especially interested in railroads.

"After the Civil War, the Central Pacific constructed almost seven-hundred miles through the Sierra to Promontory Point. That's in northern Utah. Used Chinese ruthlessly often as dynamite men, right through those mountains. All financed by the government.

The other railroad, the Union Pacific started from the Missouri River. They built over a thousand miles through the plains, also government funded. Might seem easier than the Sierra but they had harsh winters and brutal summers and Lakota and Cheyenne Indians to deal with. Took 'em seven years to Promontory and the celebration with the Golden Spike and all that. One of these days they oughta build a museum in Sacramento where the railroad ended." A fella at the end of the bar was tapping his glass with a spoon and Mike left to take his order.

Returning, Mike continued, "Those Big Four fellas have a big monopoly and big political power and wealth. Most folks think too much wealth and power. What do you fellas think? Will California be better with the railroad?"

"California might, but the Indian sure won't. We're murdering their buffalo and destroying a civilization. There were once maybe sixty million buffalo roaming the plains. A sad end of a story, a sad end of a people. But I don't have any answers."

The American buffalo or bison had roamed freely on the Great Plains since the last Ice Age ten thousand years back. The mass slaughter and near extinction was made possible by the railroad.

After President Lincoln signed the Railway Act of 1862, railroad financier, George Francis Train proclaimed: *The great Pacific Railway has commenced…Immigration will soon pour into these valleys. Ten millions of immigrants will settle in this Golden Land in twenty years…This is the grandest enterprise under God!*

The next morning, the cousins after paying the hotel, found a carriage that took them to the stables.

"King Caleb, where now."

"Seems only one way left for us."

"And that seems to be north."

"Seems."

CHAPTER TEN

Early December was wet and cold, their ponchos and sombreros protecting as best they could. After leaving The City, they returned to clothes more befitting vaqueros.

Riding through forests, gentle hills and more forests every few days, then turning to the sea, they found a beautiful deserted coast with an occasional small fishing village. Diego was supporting them with protein from the sea. Fires were hard to keep going with the deadfall mostly wet. If they rode into the forest, they found enough wood kept dry by the canopy. A deer from Caleb's Henry fed them as well. They couldn't make jerky, but they smoked enough to keep them going.

"Think we'll know when we reach Oregon, cousin?"

"Don't know when California ends and Oregon starts, hoping for a settlement soon and ask some folks. Might ride all the way to the North Pole if we're not careful."

Trying to keep each other's moods bright they joked and joshed each other.

"You broke your promise, Diego."

"How did I do that, haven't made you any, at least that I remember."

"You said I could be Buffalo Hump."

"Ha, what made you think of that?"

"There's some Indios up the way."

"I see them now, at least I see some smoke from a few places, maybe a village."

They were Yurok, a dozen men camped smoking fish hanging from racks. Shunning the cousins, they acted as if they were invisible.

Acting on an impulse, Caleb brought out a leg of venison from his pack and presented the gift to an older man and in a moment a smile from a mouth mostly empty of teeth.

The Yurok knew some Spanish and they communicated as best they could. The Indian invited them to eat dried fish with them. It was the friendly exchange of gifts. The boys learned they were at what the Yurok called Duluwat and they called their village Tolowot. As the Indians continued their chores, the old man explained to them of Uytaahkoo, a white mountain that reached into the sky a month's walk east from Tolowot. The Indian also talked of mighty trees a ten-days walk north and the home of ghosts. He had never been there but knew they must be homes of ghosts if not gods.

Diego and Caleb signed their goodbyes, deciding to take a look first at the trees.

"The old Indian was right, Caleb, these are mighty. Similar to those Sequoias Cole showed us above Yosemite and it's quiet, silent in here."

"Take a look at the bark here, really fibrous and red. And those dead vines. Blackberry bushes all over, could have a feast in the summer. Let's ride for a couple days and find out how big this forest is."

"Almost like church in here, Caleb. Would be church to Mr. Muir. He must know about these don't you think. When we get back to the ranch, let's write him a letter, address it, Mr. John Muir, The City, that'll find him. And our dads could write some words too."

"Wondering Diego, if one of these trees fell over and no one was here, would it make any noise?"

Mostly making their own path, sometimes following Indian trails, they drifted south and east. And then in a week Uytaahkoo, the white mountain. They were stunned by the view.

"Does, it reaches the sky, and that mountain sure holds a lot of snow, Diego."

"There's someone in the river ahead, Caleb."

"Might know something."

"I'll be, two cowboys or vaqueros. Howdy, get off those nags. I got coffee to share. Haven't talked English or Mexican for some time. Which do you prefer?"

"'No importa' from Caleb and 'Doesn't matter' from Diego.

"Well English is easier for me, how 'bout that?"

They followed their new friend a mile to his camp.

"Name's Peterson. Folks who know me call me Butch, forgot why.

Drink up, got plenty of this coffee. My first question, what you two doin' up here?"

"We're tourists, Butch. Need to see what's over that next hill. We fish, hunt a little and when we need, we work for a time. And your second question?"

"How long you been away?"

"About a year and a half."

"And you Butch, what's your story?"

"Lemme get some sticks here for the fire, git more of this coffee goin'. Got some venison be happy to share. Valleys rich with deer and elk. Got some beaver too. Plenty fish in the rivers, a real paradise unless you need folks. And then there's the mountain. Ol' Shasta watches over me, makes me feel kinda special. Do have some skeeters, smoke from the fire helps. Indians keep damp logs smolderin' to keep them bugs calm. Indians hunt here too but no permanent village, gotta head north a few days for Klamath, that's 'bout where Oregon starts.

Don't do much, trap a little and trade the pelts for what I need, not much. Just never had ambition but to live outdoors. Have a couple of wives, a Yurok and a Klamath, both fine ladies. For some reason they think I'm too lazy for them."

"Would that be an old Hawkins in that leather sleeve, Butch, fifty-four caliber."

"Is, but how would a young fella like you know 'bout breechloaders?"

"Got one at home. It's my dad's, used it when he came west from Colorado about forty-seven or forty-eight. Rode out here with my Uncle Noah, Caleb's dad."

"Where in Colorado? Had family there once."

"Dads came from San Luis, it's the oldest community ever in the Territory. Both think Colorado's going be a state in a couple years. They think they'll call it the Centennial State since it's been a hundred years since America was ours."

"Well now, that deserves a splash of my best, oughta git started on the celebration. Here's a couple tin cups. Washed 'em just last year," Butch grinned. "This here whiskey's powerful. Help yourself but be forewarned."

Diego picked up the jug and poured some mash in Butch's cup. Butch was a good host, entertaining his guests with his favorite stories between sips.

"Jim Colter left the Lewis and Clark expedition just 'fore it returned to St. Louis. Jim was one of them first real Mountain Men, a trapper and trader, explored all through them Rockies. That 'ol boy found that place with them geysers and gasses sneakin' out of the ground, called it Colter's Hell. Oughta save places like that alone so folks don' ruin it. Seemed Jim's luck ran out when the Blackfeet got 'em. They killed his pard, John Potts. Don' know why, but they decided to have a little sport with Jim, so them Indians stripped him bare-ass, gave him a head start and tol' him to run. Jim ran and ran, hid in them icy-cold beaver dams and eleven days and some two hundred miles later stumbled onto Fort Raymond. Lil' more of that whiskey Diego, oughta improve my memory some. Got 'nother jug 'round here someplace, mebbe under them pelts over there. Now, where was I?"

"Coulter had run to Fort Raymond."

"Right. Raymond, that's the fort where the Bighorn and Yellowstone meet. Well after some time, Jim left the mountains, married and farmed then joined that 1812 war, died of yellow jaundice. You boys lookin' a little sleepy-eyed, got just one more for ya. Have more of this jerky helps the whisky go down.

You heard 'bout that grizzly Hugh Glass surprised with her cubs? Well That brown ripped ol' Hugh to pieces. After a couple days of carrying him, his partners both left him for dead, took his kit, knife and Hawkin."

"They left Hugh Glass behind for dead?"

"Did. Took Hugh some time all crippled up like that to crawl more than two hundred miles hiding from them Arikaras the whole time. All that with a broken leg he set right hisself, open chest wounds all festerin', back to the trappers who had given up on him at Fort Kiowa on the Missouri."

The three woke late with bad heads and thick mouths. It was raining.

"No offence boys, but I'm glad I don't have too many visitors like you. Do remember you inviting me to Sonoma to visit, might try to do that, just might."

During a breakfast of venison and beans, both cold, Butch asked, "You goin' to see the lava beds country? Probably less than two-hundred miles. If you're here to see something special, that's one's special for sure. Lemme make some coffee and I'll tell ya 'bout Captain Jack.

Called the Modoc Wars, only heard of one other Indian war ever in California, on the other side of them Sierra. Some Modocs up there wanted to leave the reservation. And of course, the government didn't want 'em to leave. Careful these cups get hot. When I was livin' with the Klamath, heard 'bout most of what went on. War just over earlier this year. You'll like these, names: Kintpuash, Scarface Charley, and Shaknasty Jim, those boys were the leaders of the Modoc. Reckon one hundred twenty warriors fought one thousand infantry counting scouts and volunteers.

Put a couple those sticks on the fire, will ya, Caleb. Forgot where I was."

"The soldiers who were fighting."

"Right. Well the lava beds were hard for the regular army to fight in, its Modoc country. Finally, a peace conference and Kintpuash, that's Captain Jack to most people, well he killed a General Edward Canby and a preacher, Eleazar Thomas. Like I said, after most a year the army captures Jack. He's the only Indian leader ever to be charged with a war crime. Well, they hung him and three other warriors. The rest of the Modoc fighters sent to Oklahoma. There's still plenty of other Modoc up there.

Tell ya' what, I'll join ya', haven't seen those lava beds in a while. Gotta find my horse, he's out there somewhere, doesn't seem to roam too far."

"Nice to have a guide, Butch." They were climbing into very broken ground. A misstep could easily snap a horse's leg. Dismounting they led their mounts through the most difficult.

"Just before sundown, we might see a whole lotta bats. Lots of caves, never been in one, but a whole lotta bats most nights."

Now and then they'd meet solemn, sad looking Indians. "Interesting Butch but not a happy place, the land looks sad and the Indians sadder."

The cousins decided to ride to Oregon from Modoc country. Butch wanted to visit the Klamath camp to visit one of his wives.

"Straight north and you're bound to run into Oregon. Have a look and drop by my camp for a few days on the way back if you're goin' home that way. Got another story or two."

CHAPTER ELEVEN

Diego and Caleb rode into Sonoma two years after they left.

"What do you think cousin, maybe a bath and a barber?"

"Better, don't want to scare the folks. Do we arrive as vaqueros? Or wear our Stanford outfits?"

"I elect for vaqueros."

"Vaqueros we'll be."

Miguel saw them first, a small prayer of thanks. Then the dogs, first barking a warning then greeting their old friends, smiling with their tails. The young men rode to Caleb's home first.

At the end of the day, parents, siblings, grandparents and workers all greeted them. Diego and Caleb had become much more than boys in their nineteen years.

Three days later after Sunday's supper, the four sat on Jarrett's veranda. Diego and Caleb had shared most of their adventure during the days they were home, adding a few anecdotes at the meal.

"Got a letter here, Noah. It's from two college students looking for work this summer. Says they'll work for room and board, just want the experience. Coming by in person next week for an interview."

"You have the letter there, Jar?"

"Do, here it is. Their names are Smith and Jones."

Looking at each with crooked smiles, the sons sipped their port.

BOOK THREE

DAUGHTERS OF MEN

DAUGHTERS OF MEN

She was cruising between Vancouver and Australia in calm equatorial waters. The navigator, finishing his calculations, reported to Captain John Phillips. Their position at 0 degrees, 31 minutes north, by 179 degrees, 30 minutes west was nearing the point where the equator intersects the International Date Line. The Engine Order Telegraph sounded bells to the engine room. Captain Phillips ordered from Full Ahead to Slow Ahead to Dead Slow Ahead to Stop.

At exactly midnight on 31 December 1899, the ship lay astride the point where the two imaginary lines meet. The *SS Warrimoo* was in two different hemispheres, two different seasons, two different months, two different weeks, two different days, two different years and two different centuries all at the same time.

Four thousand four hundred forty-two miles away, Central Park was hosting a Turn of the Century party for Los Angeles.

Gabriela Andersen and her 'much older' cousin, Valentina Andersen, were taking in the celebration. Valentina was senior by three months and two days.

"Getting crazy Chica, have to yell to hear. Anything left in the bota?"

"Here you go, Tina. The mariachis are back again, wonder how many times we heard 'Cielito Lindo' tonight? And there's the Kissing Bandito making his rounds again. Think he's kinda cute?"

"Better question Gabby is how many times have you been kissed tonight, not counting our Bandito Amigo?"

Drinking, dancing, conga lines, drinking, flirting and drinking! Loud and crazy like a Turn of the Century Party oughta be.

"It'll be midnight in a few minutes Tina, I'm off to see if I can corral Roy..... there he is."

"Roy, Roy Scaffidi, over here. Wondered if you were going to make the party."

"Lucky to make it at all, tell ya later. At least I'm in time for the countdown."

The crowd in the square, realizing they were witnessing a new century started counting as nineteen hundred was introduced:

TEN, NINE, EIGHT, SEVEN, SIX, FIVE, FOUR, THREE, TWO, ONE!

Their kiss lasted much longer than the countdown, finishing one century and starting another. The folks in the square went nutso, well into the new centennial.

Tina and Roy were partial to small ethnic places for meals. At six that evening they met outside D'Auria's, a small Italian joint the aficionados wanted to keep their own. Joe D'auria's secret was his wife Florence, who personally prepared the meals. Joe provided the *personaggio*.

"Hi Favorite, you always look so darn pretty. What a time this city had last night. Glad I was able to catch a little of the celebration. I'll make up for it at the Two Thousand party."

"Just glad you made it, for the countdown Roy."

Joe greeted them with saluti amici and a belt of Campari for each of them to chase the cobwebs away."

Others were arriving for dinner and he left them with a grazie, returning a bit later for their order.

"Special request tonight Joe, bring us what you and Flo would order if you were eating Italian tonight. And pick the vino as well, please."

A couple of guys in the booth next to them were talking about the 1901 inaugural Tournament-East West Football Game in Pasadena that they had just witnessed. Michigan had defeated Stanford 49-0. The Stanford captain, Ralph Fischer, requested the game be stopped with eight minutes remaining. Coach Fielding Yost's Michigan team finished their season 11-0. Yost had been Stanford's coach the previous year.

After Roy walked Tina to her apartment, they kissed awhile and then he caught the last Yellow Trolley to his place, three miles away.

The last Spanish colonial rule in the Americas ended with the 1898 Spanish-American War and resulted in the acquisition of territories in Latin America and the Pacific. The First California Regiment served in the Philippines. The unit took part in actions near Malate and the capture of Manila. Nine hundred eighty-six enlisted men and fifty-one officers served.

Then Tecumseh struck again! William McKinley, elected in 1900 was assassinated in Buffalo, New York. He now joined Harrison, elected-1840, Lincoln-1860 and Garfield-1880, each a generation apart. Who might be next?

Phineas Banning and John Downey in 1869, were the power behind laying the city's first rails of twenty-one miles between Los Angeles and San Pedro. Meanwhile, the port of San Pedro was excavated into a harbor more inviting for tankers, freighters and cruise liners. Los Angeles was joining the world.

The Central Pacific from San Francisco and the Santa Fe and Southern Pacific from the East joined the rush, stimulating economic growth. Tourists poured in by the thousands. Then the Southern Pacific connected from San Francisco opening the north for more commerce and travel.

Oil, another industry, would soon be needing the rails. It sprang to life after discovery in 1892 near present day Dodger Stadium. Many fields close by, soon supplied the world with twenty-five per cent of its supply. Little did they know that also in 1902, the first production motor car was built with one cylinder on Main Street and would evolve into a machine that would demand gasoline, a by-product of that oil.

Evolving from a settlement of forty-four original *Pobladores*, Los Angeles now hosted one hundred three thousand. And the century had just begun.

Valentina and Roy married in June of 1902 and rented a place in Echo Park across from the lake. Cousin Gabriela and Thom married soon after settling in Long Beach. The Pacific Electric Railway's Red cars connected the Echo Park area with Long Beach allowing the easy transit of twenty-three miles. The families experienced the Southland's growth through the years.

Dear Valentina,

Can you believe, it's been almost a year for both of us. Let's all get together Saturday. Choose some place.

We like everything and Roy and I'll meet you at Echo Park. Are those geese at the park still mean?

Don Aikens, the boy next door, is attending the University of Southern California. He's even on the football team. Don told me the school won their first football game back in '88, 16-0 over the Alliance Club. He showed me a pamphlet, says USC opened its doors in '80 and cost fifteen dollars a term. Affiliated with the Methodist Church, it started with fifty-three students and a faculty of ten. Its first class in '84 graduated three, one a female, Minnie Miltimore, the class valedictorian. Yay for her!

I wonder if L.A. will ever be big enough to have a school like Cal Berkeley?

PS. Don told me he had a girlfriend, Marge. Said she was perfect except she didn't like football.

Gabby

Celebrating their first anniversary together, the four friends rode the trolley to Olvera Street and walked the two blocks into Chinatown. At Foo Chow, a new Cantonese restaurant, they had a more serious evening than what they had planned.

"Chinatown is always fun but maybe it's my social conscience. This little 'town' all came about because these folks were forced here. The newspapers seem to always be stirring people up with stories how the Chinese, and the Japanese too, are stealing jobs from white people. Sorry to get on my soapbox."

"What you say is true, Val. I remember reading that back in '71, it's called the Chinese Massacre, a mob of five hundred robbed, beat and murdered eighteen Chinese. The guilty all had their convictions overturned.

To be fair, people in a strange land would probably pick a place where their language and customs are shared. If I was going to live in Canton, I'd choose some place where I was comfortable and could speak English or Spanish."

Then their meal arrived. Tuesday was a slow night and the proprietor Yue was asked to sit with them and share a drink as they finished their steamed pudding cake.

Gabby explained, "It's our first time here and we want to say thank you. Cantonese food is special to us as we have grandfathers who spent some time in your city many years ago."

Finishing their bottle of Baijiu, Roy, who was always straightforward, asked if the exclusion law made it difficult to do business in Los Angeles. The federal Chinese Exclusion Act of 1882 was the first U.S. law implemented to prevent all members of a specific ethnic or national group from immigrating into the United States.

"We Chinese have found American 'silent partners' who help us set things in motion."

It was Thom's turn to ask, "Wouldn't blame you if you had a name not flattering for America."

"On the contrary, we have named you the 'United States of Beauty, Advantage and Endurance.' If we Chinese, or anyone different are going to be successful and fulfilled, we must do the work ourselves. I appreciate your sympathy, but victimhood is exactly what will keep us behind.

Confucius, our most honored sage, said that 'an individual without a sense of shame was no longer human', I humbly offer that people must earn respect. We Chinese must teach our children that they are responsible for themselves. White America owes them nothing except to be equal under the law. That way they will earn respect for themselves and not be victims.

If you lived in China, you would find us to be people who think ourselves most superior."

Walking back to their trolley stop, they all agreed that now they had two favorites, D'Auria's and Foo Chow.

Dear Gabby,

Hope all is well with you and Thom and the niños.
Time for us to meet for lunch, been over a month.

How about Philippe's for one of those French Dips?
My mouth is watering already.

Have you been reading about the bombing of the
Times? And two weeks later the iron works near
the plaza! Clarence Darrow is going to defend the
bombers. He was the lawyer from Chicago in that
Monkey Trial over evolution. Don't know where I
stand on that open or close shop issue.

Please let me know about lunch, Val

PS. Gotta make plans to see the folks.

Democrat William Jennings Bryan, a three-time presidential
candidate and Socialist Eugene Debs, who ran for president from
prison, championed populist and progressive theories. Republican
President Theodore Roosevelt became increasingly progressive with
his Square Deal policy. Encouraged by this political climate, the
Industrial Workers of the World had made significant progress with
longshoremen. As a result, twelve hundred 'radicals' were locked up
in Griffith Park, the gift of Col. Griffith J. Griffith, a hugely successful
mining investor.

The park of 3,015 acres, five times the size of New York's Central
Park, was Griffith Griffith's hope to open the heavens to the common
folks with an observatory, a planetarium and an amphitheater he
wanted named the Greek Theater. His legacy was marred when he
served two years in San Quentin for shooting his wife in the head at
the Arcadia hotel, leaving her disfigured with a loss of her right eye.
She survived and divorced him. Today the urban park is popular
for its rugged trails, a zoo and the Gene Autry Western Heritage
Museum. There is no evidence that the colonel was ever a colonel.
He may have been a major of rifle practice.

The game of rounders had been played in England since the time
of the Tudors. In 1744, Jane Austen referred to what would become
our national pastime in her book, *Northanger Abbey*: *It was not very
wonderful that Catherine, who had nothing heroic about her, should prefer*

cricket, baseball, riding on horseback, and running about the country at fourteen, to books.

Abner Doubleday was a U.S. Army major general who fired the first shot in the in the defense of Fort Sumpter, the opening battle of the civil war. He is the supposed inventor of the game of baseball in Elihu Phinney's cow pasture in Cooperstown, New York, in 1839. The National Baseball Hall of Fame resides where this legendary myth began. 'But don't let the truth get in the way of a good story' was the mantra of Major League Baseball.

Professional baseball came to California in 1903 and the Los Angeles Angels played in the Pacific Coast League along with the San Francisco Seals, Sacramento Senators, Oakland Oaks, Portland Beavers, and the Seattle Indians. The inaugural 1903 season contested over two hundred games for each team. The Angels finished the season in first place with a 133-78 record.

Dear Val,

Just a quick note to let you know how much Roy, the kids and I appreciated your and Thom's generosity at D'Auria's last Saturday. We're all partial to Italian, of course the kids never experiment. Spaghetti and meatballs every time. Everything on the menu is good, Joe's fun and that Florence is a gem. Roy suggested we meet at your place next Saturday and go watch that new motion picture, *In Old California.* Heard its short, not sure how long. It'll be a new experience for all of us. Can you imagine? The Yellow Car can take us there from your place. Do you think moving pictures are a passing fad? Let's go after to one of those new jazz clubs that I hear are opening up and down Broadway.

That Los Angeles river is still acting up with floods again this year. After years of drought, the ranchers and farmers move too close to the water only to be swept away by those ferocious storms. Something has to be done!

Love and kisses from us all, Gabby

PS. Heard from the folks, as I'm sure you have. They're sending us each a crate of vino and they're all well. Should have started the letter with that. I miss them!

Harrison Otis and Harry Chandler started buying cheap land in the San Fernando Valley in 1899. William Mulholland, chief engineer of the Los Angeles Department of Water and Power was enlisted in a scheme. They knew that a dry southland was stagnant but with ample water there were fortunes to be made. J. B. Lippencott surveyed the Owens Valley, persuading the valley farmers and local water companies to surrender their water rights of 200,000 acres to Fred Eaton, a former mayor of Los Angeles. Lippencott worked for the U.S. Reclamation Service and was secretly receiving a salary from the city of Los Angeles. The world's longest aqueduct was being planned.

The *Times* created an atmosphere of crisis, while available water was secretly run into sewers to generate an artificial drought. Twenty-two million dollars of bonds were voted to construct a two hundred thirty-three mile watercourse from the Owens Valley to the city of Los Angeles. Beginning work in 1908, the Los Angeles Aqueduct started delivering water in 1913.

Dear Gabby,

Can you believe it, five words! Mulholland's whole speech only five words. Thom says it's the most important event that has ever happened to the city. 'There it is. Take it.' Five words! Thom and I go back and forth about honor and all that. Maybe that's a question for future generations to answer.

Bring your gang and visit us this weekend, we've plenty room if we put the kids outside on the back lawn, they can sleep in our tent. We can all go to the beach.

Gotta go, Val

PS. How did you like the vino? Got an idea, tell ya later.

Back in the 1840's, downtown Los Angeles was the site of the first citrus farm. William Wolfskill started it all, ignited by the huge demand for oranges by gold rushers to combat scurvy. Securing his seedlings from the San Gabriel Mission, it was not until the introduction of the seedless Brazilian navel orange, so called because the end of the fruit resembles a belly button, that citrus became king. Its kingdom: Los Angeles, Orange and Riverside Counties. And the Screwdriver had yet to be invented!

In the early 1900s, most motion picture patents were held by Thomas Edison in New Jersey. Makers of films moved to West Los Angeles to evade his patents.

During the Mexican-American War, the 1831 Battle of Cahuenga Pass was fought very near where, in 1912, D. W. Griffith would direct *In Old California*. Griffith's motion picture, a seventeen-minute silent film, established the industry. The weather and territory a bonus.

HOLLYWOODLAND, the original sign, was erected in 1923 by *Los Angeles Times* publisher and real estate developer, Harry Chandler to advertise his new housing development in the hills. All thirteen letters were thirty feet wide and forty-three feet tall and attached to telephone poles.

> *The central figure in the seal of California is the presiding goddess of that state…But the constitution limits the franchise and thus makes outlaws of all the noble women who endured the hardships …who helped make California all that it is… the position of the real woman who shares the everyday trials and hardships… inspires no corresponding admiration and respect.*

Elizabeth Cady Stanton, 1876

Valentina and Gabriela met at the Grand Central Market two hours before noon.

"On the Red Car coming here, most men and the women knew what I was up to. These rolled up signs are a pretty good hint. Some, not all, but most I think, gave me little nods of understanding. Gave me some confidence. Two men gave me insulting stares and talked between themselves, obviously disapproving democracy and I told them so."

"Thom and I talked of course more than a few times and he'll vote for suffrage. Told me, 'Hell, women are people too and our brains wouldn't do worse than a lot of men he's heard through the years.'"

The cousins met Roy and Thom at D'Auria's at six. Joe gave them their favorite booth in the back by the kitchen.

"I think our ladies did themselves proud, Thom."

"That they did, first let me pour and then a toast to our savvy suffragists. Welcome to the fight for full-fledged citizenship."

"We learned a lot from our sisters in England and the cities back East, don't you think, Val? There were only a few rowdy men today giving us a bad time."

"The police were inept and insulted us a few times."

"What hurts is that most of our women are lethargic."

Flo came to say hello and asked some questions about the day. It was an hour early for the rush and they made room at the table for her to sit.

"*Grazie*, you are brave to do what you do, and I am proud to be la donna! If you have an extra sign, I'll put it on the wall."

"How does Joe feel about this, Flo?"

"From the start, maybe two years ago, Joe, who honors his mother back home so very much said that if he could vote he would vote for women."

"You two aren't citizens? Never thought about you that way, just took it for granted."

"We take our examination before the vote, so that is good. Our children give us tests and are bene teachers of United States la storia."

The food arrived without a bill.

All *men* are created equal had been taken literally by the U.S. Supreme Court. To win the franchise, suffragists began a nationwide campaign in 1848 to earn their civil rights and did not reach their goal until 1920. In the Golden State, a progressive Republican administration was persuaded to place the question on the ballot in 1910.

Suffragists held mass rallies, spoke to congregations, and to voters on the street, addressed unions, factory workers, any audience they could find.

The general attitude towards women voting was indifference and amusement rather than hostility. Several days after the vote, the final tally for equal suffrage was 125,037 to 121,450, passing by 3,587 votes, an average majority of only one vote per precinct in the whole Golden State.

Japanese started immigrating to California in significant numbers following political, social and cultural changes stemming from the 1868 Meiji Restoration and emerged from isolation following Mathew Perry's 1853 expedition where the commodore sailed gunships into Tokyo Bay negotiating, with force, a treaty opening trade with the reclusive nation. The Japanese suffering from high unemployment pushed economically motivated folks to seek elsewhere for a better life. The Hawaiian Islands, Washington, Oregon and California were their destinations.

The Chinese Exclusion Act prohibited Chinese to immigrate, so Japanese workers were sought for cheap labor.

The 'Land of Promise' suggested an opportunity for boys not first sons. Japan, a bit smaller than California, used the system of primogeniture as a method of inheritance which allowed only the first-born son to inherit. Without primogeniture, Japan's farms would end up the size of postage stamps in a few generations. Staying in the motherland, second and third born sons might become priests or military men. Most Japanese immigrants in California became farmers and fishermen.

Because of the rapid growth of workers, anti-Japanese sentiment increased and to prevent a crisis, Japan and the United States made a 'Gentleman's Agreement' in 1907, where Japan denied passports to people who wanted to work in the U.S. and America would allow students, business people and spouses of people already in the United States.

Little Tokyo became a thriving center of businesses, residencies and schools. The Japanese newspaper, the *Rafu Shimpo,* founded in

1903, has been in constant circulation, except for the internment years, 1942 to 1946 ever since.

"My name is Yoshio Nakamura. I have seen you a few times in the market here and wanted to meet you and there is no one to introduce me but me, so hello."

"I have seen you here at the Central Market a few times as well, Yoshio."

"I am from the machi of Tonda, it is a port in the South."

"My father has a friend he met on the boat coming over from Honolulu who is from Tokuyama. Oh, sorry, my name is Aiko Shinoda, I must deliver these vegetables now, but if you happen to be at the Kame restaurant on East First Street this Sunday at six o'clock, we could say hello again and you could meet my parents."

"This Sunday is the fourth of July, America's Independence Day, so I will not be working."

"How do you feel about America, Yoshio? My father and his friends call it, not uncomplimentary, the Rice Country."

"Of course, I have thought about this and feel like Japan is my mother and America, my father."

They met again on Sunday......

Filipinos or 'Luzon Indios' first set foot in California in 1587 at Moro Bay. They were sailors from the Spanish galleon *Nuestra Señora de Esperanza* and became the first Asians, other than Indians, to set foot in California.

Annexing the Philippines from Spain after the Spanish American War, Filipinos became United States Nationals and constitute the largest Asian-American population in California at one and a half million. Because most of the *Pinoys* came to work in the fields of the Central Valley, Little Manila in Stockton became the center of Filipino-American life.

Of the 3,464 Medal of Honor recipients, thirty-three have been earned by Asian-Americans. The first Asian-American to win the medal was Jose B. Nesperos, who received it for his actions in the Philippine-American War.

Dear Val,

How are you today, mi prima? A couple of things to share. Some folks in L.A. have gone all weird. Hope my ink doesn't run out with this name, the Divine Order of the Royal Arms of the Great Eleven is a newer cult that knows how to reveal hidden gold and to resurrect the dead. Seems to be the newest of many sects growing in our southland. Heard it has 100 members and the women even sacrifice mules. Takes all kinds!

As you know, our moms and dads go to that Big Game every year. They've turned our dads into Stanford fans and They've been going since the rivalry started in '92. USC is playing Stanford here and the folks are taking the train and have reservations at the Pico House. Our gramps saw the hotel when it was first built. Don't tell them, but Thom and I are fans of the USC 'Methodists'. Mom wrote they have a surprise for us???

Love from your 'much younger but wiser' prima, Gabby

PS. Just kidding

The Stanford Indians won the 1912 contest 14-0 at the USC Methodist's home field at Washington Park. After the game, the folks settled on the top floor of the Pico House along with their surprise, Jarrett, Yolanda, Noah and Francisca. Rooms had been reserved for Gabriela and Thom and Valentina and Roy as well. Meeting at the hotel, the family walked to D'Auria's where they had a reserved table from eight until ten o'clock.

Joe had their table scattered with bottles of Bellini Chianti straw bottle table wine and after sparring over Sonoma wine and Italy's best, the family ordered what Joe suggested: Insalata, spaghetti and meat balls and tiramisu, finishing with a little sambuca for digestion.

During dinner, Molly was asked about a novel she was writing.

"It's still a little rough, but it takes place in the early days of

Stanford, a romance between a female engineering student who falls in love with a cowboy from Colorado. No one would ever believe that," with a wink at Diego. She had just published a short story about The Yellow Peril, exposing nativist xenophobia prevalent in California.

Addy was the city engineer for the city of Santa Rosa, busy designing roads and other infrastructure projects. As a Sierra Club member, she had been actively opposing the damming of Hetch Hetchy.

"I realize San Francisco is nervous, as the fire was the scariest part of the earthquake. But as Muir explains there are other alternatives, other canyons that can be used as reservoirs to protect The City. After all, Hetch Hetchy is part of Yosemite National Park and therefore protected. Can you imagine drowning Yosemite Valley? Then Congress got involved and President Wilson signed a bill to dam the valley just last year."

The cousins asked about their brothers and their kids who were roaming the hills of the ranch, chasing that elusive Buffalo Hump, most often late for dinner.

"Suppose earthquakes are part of California living, and San Francisco seems right in harm's way so close to that San Andreas fault. That professor from Cal figured that fault stuff out ten years back."

"Thom and I often wonder what's worse, tornadoes or hurricanes or snow and ice in the East. Maybe no place is paradise. Even with quakes and wildfires, California comes darn close as far as we're concerned."

Back at the Pico House, on the top floor veranda overlooking Olvera Plaza, the family was still catching up. Noah had read Zane Grey's novel, *Riders of the Purple Sage* and Edgar Rice Burroughs, *Tarzan of the Apes*, both new 1912 novels.

Gabby and Tina cornered the dads. "Always been a bit curious. Did you two dads or grand dads ever consider the Yukon and that Klondike gold rush? That must have been ninety-six to ninety-nine."

"Noah and I talked about it, not too seriously and we remembered an old friend, a Señor Nieto who told us when we first got to California that riches were family. Thinking that over, we considered ourselves already wealthy indeed."

"And Diego and I as well. The winery was just starting and to tell the truth we didn't want to leave your moms. Don't know if we would have been tough enough, growing up in this California weather."

"If the four of us were seventeen again and hadn't met our ladies, who knows?"

"Remember when Tina and I first approached you about travelling south to L.A. We heard all your talk about seeing the elephant and we wanted to see it for ourselves. You surprised us both when you agreed it was a good thing, you called it stretching our wings. Moms weren't so sure."

"Do remember, but Caleb and I didn't know stretching your wings meant flying away and staying."

"Which ended up a good thing, Diego."

"Did, Caleb, it did."

"Times have changed my girl since you two went south, the train we took here was faster and easier than when you two left from Sacramento back in the late 90s."

"Remember Tina, that bumpy old Butterfield stage we rode?"

"Not fondly, but it did get us here. How fast did we go? Five miles an hour maybe. Made about sixty to seventy miles in a day."

"And Dad, we got really lucky and found jobs right away, both of us working for the telephone company. And then I met a man named Roy Scaffidi."

"And I hooked on to Thom."

"Reckon you'll both stay down south?"

"I know Gabby loves Long Beach, right, Prima?"

"We do like the Southland, Roy works close to home, the schools are good, and we love la playa. How 'bout your familia, Val?"

"Not sure we'll live in the city. Thought about moving to Bunker Hill but that new neighborhood's a little too chic for us with all those stately Victorian mansions and Angels Flight makes it easy to get downtown to the Central Market. Thom's been offered a good job in Burbank. That's a couple miles northwest of Griffith Park. A new aircraft company is starting up, and Thom says it would be good to grow in a new industry. Tell the truth, don't know if you'll get me in one of those air machines."

The daughters kissed the dads and left to visit the moms.

Jarrett looking down at the plaza, "Remember our ten cent beers, Noah?"

Diego chimed in with, "Caleb and I never found out what comes first, the salt or the lime?"

Fathers and sons were reminding each other about Olvera Street and their time there, a generation apart. Gabriela and Valentina were chatting with the mothers.

"We have to make this a tradition, let's trade off every other year. Next season we can meet in San Francisco. We can train back and forth using a football game as an excuse to keep this famalia together. Maybe even trade our kids for summer vacations."

With their own secret smiles, the ladies toasted each other with glasses of tawny port from a bottle with an image of a sling shot on the label.

AFTERWORD

From the State of California Native American Heritage Commission: 'Despite romantic portraits of California missions, they were essentially coercive religious, labor camps organized primarily to benefit the colonizers. The overall plan was to first militarily intimidate the local Indians with armed Spanish soldiers who always accompanied the Franciscans in their missionary efforts. At the same time, the newcomers introduced domestic stock animals that gobbled up native foods and undermined the free or "gentile" tribe's efforts to remain economically independent. A well-established pattern of bribes, intimidation and the expected onslaught of European diseases insured experienced missionaries that eventually desperate parents of sick and dying children and many elders would prompt frightened Indian families to seek assistance from the newcomers who seemed to be immune to the horrible diseases that overwhelmed Indians. The missions were authorized by the crown to "convert" the Indians in a ten-year period. Thereafter they were supposed to surrender their control over the mission's livestock, fields, orchards and building to the Indians. But the padres never achieved this goal and the lands and wealth was stolen from the Indians. The discovery of gold in the foothills of the Sierra Nevada at a sawmill construction site developed by Indian Agent Johann Sutter, ushered in one of the darkest episodes of dispossession widespread sexual assault and mass murder against the native people of California. Sutter immediately negotiated a treaty with the chief of the Coloma Nisenan Tribe which would have given a three-year lease to lands surrounding the gold discovery site. During those negotiations, the chief prophetically warned Sutter that the yellow metal he so eagerly sought was, "very bad medicine. It belonged to a demon who devoured all who searched for it." Eventually the military governor refused to endorse Sutter's self-serving actions.

Government developed economic development plans have a history of nearly a century of total failure. Currently more than thirty reservations and rancherias have established gaming businesses on their lands. Some are highly successful while other are not. Some public opposition to these activities seems to center around the fear that Indians may be cheated by their business partners. Such fears smack of paternalism and ignore the reality that few if any valuable resources can be found on Indian lands. Few private investors have come forward to work with Indian tribes outside of the gaming industry. With few choices, wise reservation leadership view gaming as an interim step toward greater economic independence. The Viejas Band of Kumeyaay Indians are the best example of how that dream can be achieved'.

LOS ANGELES SPORTS HISTORY 1860 -1986

1860 – Bull & bear fighting outlawed. First baseball game played.

1871 – First roller-skating rink opens.

1879 – The Los Angeles Athletic Club is founded.

1889 – First college football game is played between St. Vincents (Loyola) and USC.

1890 – First Tournament of Roses included chariot races.

1892 – Original Los Angeles Angels baseball team plays in the four-team California League.

1893 – Los Angeles Angels play Stockton in the first ever nighttime exhibition game on the Pacific Coast at Athletic Park.

1899 – An elevated bicycle path is constructed between Los Angeles and Pasadena.

The Southern California Golf Association is founded.

1900 – Riverside Golf Course at Griffith Park is opened, the first municipal park in the nation.

1902 – The first Tournament of Roses football game is played between Stanford and Michigan. The game is so one sided that another isn't restaged until fourteen years later.

1903 – Los Angeles joins the Pacific Coast League with the debut of the Los Angeles Angels baseball team.

1906 – First Los Angeles to Honolulu Trans-Pacific yacht race.

1907 - George Feeth introduces surfing at Redondo Beach.

1909 – The Pacific League introduces the Vernon Tigers baseball team. The city allows alcohol sales that were then banned in L.A.

1916 – The Tournament of Roses abandons chariot racing and reintroduces college football. Washington State takes revenge on the east beating Brown University 14-0.

1921 – Chewing gum magnate William K. Wrigley Jr., owner of the Chicago Cubs, buys the Pacific League Los Angeles Angels.

1922 – The Rose Bowl is completed.

1923 – The Memorial Coliseum at Exposition Park opens.

1927 – Los Angeles Open Golf Tournament is founded.

George Young of Canada completes the first successful solo Catalina Island to mainland swim in fifteen hours and forty-four minutes. Less than a month later, Myrtle Huddleston, with a time of twenty hours and forty-two minutes becomes the first woman to complete the same swim.

1928 – USC Trojans win their first national football championship.

1929 – First USC – UCLA football contest, USC 76-0.

1932 – The X Olympiad is held hosting thirty-seven nations.

1934 – Santa Anita Park opens offering a purse of one hundred thousand dollars. The opening draws 34,269 race fans.

1938 – Babe Didrikson becomes the first and only woman to ever compete in a men's PGA Tournament, the Los Angeles Open at Griffith Park.

1939 – Duke University's undefeated season of not once being scored upon comes to an end when USC scores a last-minute touchdown and wins the Rose Bowl game 7-0.

1940 – Seabiscuit wins his final race at Santa Anita Park.

1942 – Security concerns over the outbreak of the war with Japan moved the Tournament of Roses to Durham, North Carolina.

1946 – The Rams football team moves from Cleveland to LA.

The Dons (All American Football Conference) also debuts.

1947 – Pasadena and UCLA's Jackie Robinson breaks through baseball's color barrier with the Brooklyn Dodgers at Ebbets Field.

1948 – 49 - Ricardo 'Pancho' Gonzales of East Los Angeles wins two consecutive U.S. Open titles and is ranked America's number one player.

1951- The Rams defeat the Cleveland Browns, 24-17 for Los Angeles first professional sports title.

1958 – The Dodgers move from Brooklyn to L.A. and play their first game against the San Francisco Giants winning 6-5 at the Memorial Coliseum. Vin Scully begins broadcasting for the Dodgers.

1960 – The Lakers move from Minneapolis.

The Chargers play one season and move to San Diego.

1961 – Gene Autry debuts his American League baseball team.

1964 – John Wooden's UCLA Bruins win their first NCAA basketball title defeating Duke University 98-83.

1966 – The El Rancho High School Dons, in nearby Pico Rivera, are crowned National High School football champs.

1984 – L.A. hosts the XXX111 Olympiad with a record one hundred forty nations attending.

1986 – The first City of Los Angeles Marathon is held.

And as heck of a lot more.....

When all this was finished, I read a quote by the playwright and novelist Max Frisch who said, "We asked for workers. We got people instead."

Santiago hangs his caps in Belmont Shore, California, spending some of his days challenging the slopes.

Lightning Source UK Ltd.
Milton Keynes UK
UKHW011842081220
374864UK00008B/451/J

9 781664 127050